Puffin

ISLAND

USA TODAY BESTSELLING AUTHOR

SARAH MORGAN

Praise for Sarah Morgan

"Uplifting, sexy and warm, Sarah Morgan's O'Neil Brothers series is perfection."
—Jill Shalvis, *New York Times* bestselling author

"Morgan's romantic page-turner will thrill readers. The well-paced narrative is humorous [and] poignant... the chemistry between the misunderstood hero and the victimized heroine is combustible [and] her storytelling rocks. Brava!"
—*RT Book Reviews*, Top Pick, on *Suddenly Last Summer*

"*Sleigh Bells in the Snow* [is] a great wintery romance with plenty of chemistry and heart...you will be swept away by the winter wonderland and steamy romance... Morgan has really shown her talent and infused so much love, both romantic and familial, into her characters that I am anxiously looking forward to what she writes in the future."
—*All About Romance*

"This touching Christmas tale will draw tears of sorrow and joy, remaining a reader favorite for years to come."
—*Publishers Weekly*, starred review, on
Sleigh Bells in the Snow

"Morgan's brilliant talent never ceases to amaze."
—*RT Book Reviews*

"[Morgan] managed to really bring everything I love about holiday romances in general into one beautiful story full of fantastic characters, steamy chemistry, and Christmas spirit. From sleigh rides to puppies, quiet time in a snowy forest to learning to ski and the scent of gingerbread—I loved every page."
—*Smexy Books* on *Sleigh Bells in the Snow*

"Each book of hers that I discover is a treat."
—Sarah Wendell, *Smart Bitches, Trashy Books*

CONTENTS

First Time In Forever

Dear Reader,

Friendships have always been important to me. Good friends enhance the happy times and cushion the bad ones, which is why when it came to planning my new contemporary romance series I decided to write about three friends.

Emily, Brittany and Skylar have been best friends for more than ten years and made a vow to help each other if they were ever in trouble. Their sanctuary when life gets tough? Castaway Cottage on beautiful Puffin Island, Maine.

I first saw puffins in the north of England many years ago and they are the most amazing and beautiful seabirds. One detail that fascinated me was that they usually return to breed on the same island where they hatched. Although they are not an endangered species, they are rare now in Maine and there are projects to reintroduce them to some of the islands.

The theme of returning home was one that I used as a thread throughout the stories. In this case the home is Castaway Cottage, a beachside retreat left to Brittany by her grandmother.

When Emily's circumstances change dramatically and she finds herself guardian to her sister's child, she turns to the sanctuary of Puffin Island. But life by the sea brings its own challenges for Emily, whose life choices were shaped by an incident in her past. She's hiding secrets, but it isn't easy keeping secrets in a close-knit community, especially when sexy yacht club owner Ryan Cooper makes it his personal mission to break down every barrier she's ever built. Soon she isn't just protecting her niece, she's protecting her heart.

These stories are about love, friendship and community. I hope you fall in love with the characters and also with the windswept beauty of Puffin Island. Head over to my website, sarahmorgan.com, to see some of my photographs of Maine and puffins, and sign up to my newsletter to be informed of future book releases. If you enjoy *First Time in Forever*, don't miss Brittany's story, *Some Kind of Wonderful*.

Thank you for reading.

Love,

Sarah

xxx

For Laura Reeth, makeup expert,
style guru and dear friend.

"We must free ourselves of the hope that the sea will ever rest. We must learn to sail in high winds."

Aristotle Onassis

CHAPTER ONE

IT WAS THE perfect place for someone who didn't want to be found. A dream destination for people who loved the sea.

Emily Donovan hated the sea.

She stopped the car at the top of the hill and turned off the headlights. Darkness wrapped itself around her, smothering her like a heavy blanket. She was used to the city, with its shimmering skyline and the dazzle of lights that turned night into day. Here, on this craggy island in coastal Maine, there was only the moon and the stars. No crowds, no car horns, no high-rise buildings. Nothing but wave-pounded cliffs, the shriek of gulls and the smell of the ocean.

She would have drugged herself on the short ferry crossing if it hadn't been for the child strapped into the seat in the back of the car.

The little girl's eyes were still closed, her head tilted to one side and her arms locked in a stranglehold around a battered teddy bear. Emily retrieved her phone and opened the car door quietly.

Please don't wake up.

She walked a few steps away from the car and dialed. The call went to voice mail.

"Brittany? Hope you're having a good time in Greece. Just wanted to let you know I've arrived. Thanks again for letting me use the cottage. I'm really... I'm—" *Grateful.* That was the word she was looking for. Grateful. She took a deep breath and closed her eyes. "I'm panicking. What the hell am I doing here? There's water everywhere and I hate water. This is— Well, it's hard." She glanced toward the sleeping child and lowered her voice. "She wanted to get out of the car on the ferry, but I kept her strapped in because there was *no way* I was doing that. That scary harbor guy with the big eyebrows probably thinks I'm insane, by the way, so you'd better pretend you don't know me next time you're home. I'll stay until tomorrow because there's no choice, but then I'm taking the first ferry out of here. I'm going somewhere else. Somewhere landlocked like...like... Wyoming or Nebraska."

As she ended the call the breeze lifted her hair, and she could smell salt and sea in the air.

She dialed again, a different number this time, and felt a rush of relief as the call was answered and she heard Skylar's breathy voice.

"Skylar Tempest."

"Sky? It's me."

"Em? What's happening? This isn't your number."

"I changed my cell phone."

"You're worried someone might trace the call? Holy crap, this is exciting."

"It's not exciting. It's a nightmare."

"How are you feeling?"

"Like I want to throw up, but I know I won't because I haven't eaten for two days. The only thing in my stomach is a knot of nervous tension."

"Have the press tracked you down?"

"I don't think so. I paid cash for everything and drove from New York." She glanced back at the road, but there was only darkness. "How do people live like this? I feel like a criminal. I've never hidden from anyone in my life before."

"Have you been switching cars to confuse them? Did you dye your hair purple and buy a pair of glasses?"

"No. Have you been drinking?"

"I watch a lot of movies. You can't trust anyone. You need a disguise. Something that will help you blend in."

"I will never blend in anywhere with a coastline. I'll be the one wearing a life jacket in the middle of Main Street."

"You're going to be fine." Skylar's extrafirm tone suggested she wasn't at all convinced by what she was saying.

"I'm leaving first thing tomorrow."

"You can't do that! We agreed the cottage would be the safest place to hide. No one is going to notice you on an island crowded with tourists. It's a dream place for a vacation."

"It's not a dream place when the sight of water makes you hyperventilate."

"You're not going to do that. You're going to breathe in the sea air and relax."

"I don't need to be here. This whole thing is an overreaction. No one is looking for me."

"You're the half sister of one of the biggest movie stars in Hollywood, and you're guardian to her child. If that little fact gets out, the whole press pack will be hunting you. You need somewhere to hide, and Puffin Island is perfect."

Emily shivered under a cold drench of panic. "Why would they know about me? Lana spent her entire life pretending I don't exist." And that had suited her perfectly. At no point had she aspired to be caught in the beam of Lana's spotlight. Emily was fiercely private. Lana, on the other hand, had demanded attention from the day she was born.

It occurred to Emily that her half sister would have enjoyed the fact she was still making headlines even though it had been over a month since the plane crash that had killed her and the man reputed to have been her lover.

"Journalists can find out anything. This is like a plot for a movie."

"No, it isn't! It's my *life*. I don't want it ripped open and exposed for the world to see and I don't—" Emily broke off and then said the words aloud for the first time. "I don't want to be responsible for a child." Memories from the past drifted from the dark corners of her brain like smoke under a closed door. "I can't be."

It wasn't fair to the girl.

And it wasn't fair to her.

Why had Lana done this to her? Was it malice? Lack of thought? Some twisted desire to seek revenge for a childhood where they'd shared nothing except living space?

"I know you think that, and I understand your reasons, but you can do this. You have to. Right now you're all she has."

"I shouldn't be all anyone has. That's a raw deal. I shouldn't be looking after a child for five minutes, let alone the whole summer."

No matter that in her old life people deferred to her, recognized her expertise and valued her judgment; in this she was incompetent. She had no qualifications that equipped her for this role. Her childhood had been about surviving. About learning to nurture herself and protect herself while she lived with a mother who was mostly absent—sometimes physically, always emotionally. And after she'd left home, her life had been about studying and working long, punishing hours to silence men determined to prove she was less than they were.

And now here she was, thrown into a life where what she'd learned counted for nothing. A life that required the one set of skills she *knew* she didn't possess. She didn't know how to be this. She didn't know how to *do* this. And she'd never had ambitions to do it. It felt like an injustice to find herself in a situation she'd worked hard to avoid all her life.

Beads of sweat formed on her forehead, and she heard Skylar's voice through a mist of anxiety.

"If having her stops you thinking that, this will turn out to be the best thing that ever happened to you. You weren't to blame for what happened when you were a child, Em."

"I don't want to talk about it."

"Doesn't change the fact you weren't to blame. And you don't need to talk about it because the way you feel is evident in the way you've chosen to live your life."

Emily glanced back at the child sleeping in the car. "I can't take care of her. I can't be what she needs."

"You mean you don't want to be."

"My life is adult-focused. I work sixteen-hour days and have business lunches."

"Your life sucks. I've been telling you that for a long time."

"I liked my life! I want it back."

"That was the life where you were working like a machine and living with a man with the emotional compass of a rock?"

"I liked my job. I knew what I was doing. I was competent. And Neil and I may not have had a grand passion, but we shared a lot of interests."

"Name one."

"I— We liked eating out."

"That's not an interest. That's an indication that you were both too tired to cook."

"We both enjoyed reading."

"Wow, that must have made the bedroom an exciting place."

Emily struggled to come up with something else and failed. "Why are we talking about Neil? That's over. My whole life now revolves around a six-year-old girl. There is a pair of fairy wings in her bag. I don't know anything about fairy wings."

Her childhood had been a barren desert, an exercise in endurance rather than growth, with no room for anything as fragile and destructible as gossamer-thin fairy wings.

"I have a vivid memory of being six. I wanted to be a ballerina."

Emily stared straight ahead, remembering how she'd felt at

the age of six. Broken. Even after she'd eventually stuck herself back together, she'd known she wasn't the same.

"I'm mad at Lana. I'm mad at her for dying and for putting me in this position. How screwed up is that?"

"It's not screwed up. It's human. What do you expect, Em? You haven't spoken to Lana in over a decade—" Skylar broke off, and Emily heard voices in the background.

"Do you have company? Did I catch you at a bad time?"

"Richard and I are off to a fund-raiser at The Plaza, but he can wait."

From what she knew of Richard's ruthless political ambitions and impatient nature, Emily doubted he'd be prepared to wait. She could imagine Skylar, her blond hair secured in an elegant twist on top of her head, her narrow body sheathed in a breathtaking designer creation. She suspected Richard's attraction to Sky lay in her family's powerful connections rather than her sunny optimism or her beauty. "I shouldn't have called you. I tried Brittany, but she's not answering. She's still on that archaeological dig in Crete. I guess it's the middle of the night over there."

"She seems to be having a good time. Did you see her Facebook update? She's up to her elbows in dirt and hot Greek men. She's working with that lovely ceramics expert, Lily, who gave me all those ideas for my latest collection. And if you hadn't called me I would have called you. I've been so worried. First Neil dumped you, then you had to leave your job, and now this! They say trouble comes in threes."

Emily eyed the child, still sleeping in the car. "I wish the third thing had been a broken toaster."

"You're going through a bad time, but you have to remember that everything happens for a reason. For a start, it has stopped you wallowing in bed eating cereal from the box. You needed a focus and now you have one."

"I didn't need a dependent six-year-old who dresses in pink and wears fairy wings."

"Wait a minute—" There was a pause and then the sound of a door clicking. "Richard is talking to his campaign manager, and I don't want them listening. I'm hiding in the bathroom. The things I do in the name of friendship. You still there, Em?"

"Where would I go? I'm surrounded by water." She shuddered. "I'm trapped."

"Honey, people pay good money to be 'trapped' on Puffin Island."

"I'm not one of them. What if I can't keep her safe, Sky?"

There was a brief silence. "Are we talking about safe from the press or safe from other stuff?"

Her mouth felt dry. "All of it. I don't want the responsibility. I don't want children."

"Because you're afraid to give anything of yourself."

There was no point in arguing with the truth.

"That's why Neil ended it. He said he was tired of living with a robot."

"I guess he used his own antennae to work that out. Bastard. Are you brokenhearted?"

"No. I'm not as emotional as you and Brittany. I don't feel deeply." But she should feel *something*, shouldn't she? The truth was that after two years of living with a man, she'd felt no closer to him than she had the day she'd moved in. Love wrecked people, and she didn't want to be wrecked. And now she had a child. "Why do you think Lana did it?"

"Made you guardian? God knows. But knowing Lana, it was because there wasn't anyone else. She'd pissed off half of Hollywood and slept with the other half, so I guess she didn't have any friends who would help. Just you."

"But she and I—"

"I know. Look, if you want my honest opinion, it was probably because she knew you would put your life on hold and do the best for her child despite the way she treated you. Whatever you think about yourself, you have a deep sense of responsibility. She took advantage of the fact you're a good, decent person. Em, I am *so* sorry, but I have to go. The car is outside and Richard is pacing. Patience isn't one of his good qualities and he has to watch his blood pressure."

"Of course." Privately Emily thought if Richard worked harder at controlling his temper, his blood pressure might follow, but she didn't say anything. She wasn't in a position to give relationship advice to anyone. "Thanks for listening. Have fun tonight."

"I'll call you later. No, wait—I have a better idea. Richard is busy this weekend, and I was going to escape to my studio, but why don't I come to you instead?"

"Here? To Puffin Island?"

"Why not? We can have some serious girl time. Hang out in our pajamas and watch movies like we did when Kathleen was alive. We can talk through everything and make a plan. I'll bring everything I can find that is pink. Get through to the weekend. Take this a day at a time."

"I am not qualified to take care of a child for five minutes, let alone five days." But the thought of getting back on that ferry in the morning made her feel almost as sick as the thought of being responsible for another human being.

"Listen to me." Skylar lowered her voice. "I feel bad speaking ill of the dead, but you know a lot more than Lana did. She left the kid alone in a house the size of France and hardly ever saw her. Just be there. Seeing the same person for two consecutive days will be a novelty. How is she, anyway? Does she understand what has happened? Is she traumatized?"

Emily thought about the child, silent and solemn-eyed. Trauma, she knew, wore different faces. "She's quiet. Scared of anyone with a camera."

"Probably overwhelmed by the crowds of paparazzi outside the house."

"The psychologist said the most important thing is to show her she's secure."

"You need to cut off her hair and change her name or something. A six-year-old girl with long blond hair called Juliet is a giveaway. You might as well hang a sign on her saying 'Made in Hollywood'"

"You think so?" Panic sank sharp claws into her flesh. "I thought coming out here to the middle of nowhere would be enough. The name isn't that unusual."

"Maybe not in isolation, but attached to a six-year-old everyone is talking about? Trust me, you need to change it. Puffin Island may be remote geographically, but it has the internet. Now go and hide out and I'll see you Friday night. Do you still have your key to the cottage?"

"Yes." She'd felt the weight of it in her pocket all the way from New York. Brittany had presented them both with a key on their last day of college. "And thanks."

"Hey." Sky's voice softened. "We made a promise, remember? We are always here for each other. Speak to you later!"

In the moment before she hung up, Emily heard a hard male voice in the background and wondered again what free-spirited Skylar saw in Richard Everson.

As she slid back into the car the child stirred. "Are we there yet?"

Emily turned to look at her. She had Lana's eyes, that beautiful rain-washed green that had captivated movie audiences everywhere. "Almost there." She tightened her grip on the wheel and felt the past rush at her like a rogue wave threatening to swamp a vulnerable boat.

She wasn't the right person for this. The right person would be soothing the girl and producing endless supplies of age-appropriate entertainment, healthy drinks and nutritious food. Emily wanted to open the car door and bolt into that soupy darkness, but she could feel those eyes fixed on her.

Wounded. Lost. Trusting.

And she knew she wasn't worthy of that trust.

And Lana had known it, too. So why had she done this?

"Have you always been my aunt?" The sleepy voice dragged

her back into the present, and she remembered that this *was* her future. It didn't matter that she wasn't equipped for it, that she didn't have a clue—she had to do it. There was no one else.

"Always."

"So why didn't I know?"

"I— Your mom probably forgot to mention it. And we lived on opposite sides of the country. You lived in LA and I lived in New York." Somehow she formed the words, although she knew the tone wasn't right. Adults used different voices when they talked to children, didn't they? Soft, soothing voices. Emily didn't know how to soothe. She knew numbers. Shapes. Patterns. Numbers were controllable and logical, unlike emotions. "We'll be able to see the cottage soon. Just one more bend in the road."

There was always one more bend in the road. Just when you thought life had hit a safe, straight section and you could hit "cruise," you ended up steering around a hairpin with a lethal tumble into a dark void as your reward for complacency.

The little girl shifted in her seat, craning her neck to see in the dark. "I don't see the sea. You said we'd be living in a cottage on a beach. You promised." The sleepy voice wobbled, and Emily felt her head throb.

Please, don't cry.

Tears hadn't featured in her life for twenty years. She'd made sure she didn't care about anything enough to cry about it. "You can't see it, but it's there. The sea is everywhere." Hands shaking, she fumbled with the buttons, and the windows slid down with a soft purr. "Close your eyes and listen. Tell me what you hear."

The child screwed up her face and held her breath as the cool night air seeped into the car. "I hear crashing."

"The crashing is the sound of the waves on the rocks." She managed to subdue the urge to put her hands over her ears. "The sea has been pounding away at those rocks for centuries."

"Is the beach sandy?"

"I don't remember. It's a beach." And she couldn't imagine herself going there. She hadn't set foot on a beach since that day when her life had changed.

Nothing short of deep friendship would have brought her to this island in the first place, and even when she'd come she'd stayed indoors, curled up on Brittany's colorful patchwork bedcover with her friends, keeping her back to the ocean.

Kathleen, Brittany's grandmother, had known something was wrong, and when her friends had sprinted down the sandy path to the beach to swim, she'd invited Emily to help her in the sunny country kitchen that overlooked the tumbling color of the garden. There, with the gentle hiss of the kettle drowning out the sound of waves, it had been possible to pretend the sea wasn't almost lapping at the porch.

They'd made pancakes and cooked them on the skillet that had once belonged to Kathleen's mother. By the time her friends returned, trailing sand and laughter, the pancakes had been piled on a plate in the center of the table—mounds of fluffy deliciousness with raggedy edges and golden warmth. They'd eaten them drizzled with maple syrup and fresh blueberries harvested from the bushes in Kathleen's pretty coastal garden.

Emily could still remember the tangy sweet flavor as they'd burst in her mouth.

"Will I have to hide indoors?" The little girl's voice cut through the memories.

"I— No. I don't think so." The questions were never-ending, feeding her own sense of inadequacy until, bloated with doubt, she could no longer find her confident self.

She wanted to run, but she couldn't.

There was no one else.

She fumbled in her bag for a bottle of water, but it made no difference. Her mouth was still dry. It had been dry since the moment the phone on her desk had rung with the news that had changed her life. "We'll have to think about school."

"I've never been to school."

Emily reminded herself that this child's life had never been close to normal. She was the daughter of a movie star, conceived during an acclaimed Broadway production of *Romeo and Juliet*. There had been rumors that the father was Lana's co-star, but as he'd been married with two children at the time, that had been vehemently denied by all concerned. They'd recently been reunited on their latest project, and now he was dead, too, killed in the same crash that had taken Lana, along with the director and members of the production team.

Juliet.

Emily closed her eyes. *Thanks, Lana.* Sky was right. She was going to have to do something about the name. "We're just going to take this a day at a time."

"Will he find us?"

"He?"

"The man with the camera. The tall one who follows me everywhere. I don't like him."

Cold oozed through the open windows, and Emily closed them quickly, checking that the doors were locked.

"He won't find us here. None of them will."

"They climbed into my house."

Emily felt a rush of outrage. "That won't happen again. They don't know where you live."

"What if they find out?"

"I'll protect you."

"Do you promise?" The childish request made her think of Skylar and Brittany.

Let's make a promise. When one of us is in trouble, the others help, no questions.

Friendship.

For Emily, friendship had proven the one unbreakable bond in her life.

Panic was replaced by another emotion so powerful it shook her. "I promise." She might not know anything about being a mother and she might not be able to love, but she *could* stand between this child and the rest of the world.

She'd keep that promise, even if it meant dying her hair purple.

"I SAW LIGHTS in Castaway Cottage." Ryan pulled the bow line tight to prevent the boat moving backward in the slip. From up above, the lights from the Ocean Club sent fingers of gold dancing across the surface of the water. Strains of laughter and music floated on the wind, mingling with the call of seagulls. "Know anything about that?"

"No, but I don't pay attention to my neighbors the way you do. I mind my own business. Did you try calling Brittany?"

"Voice mail. She's somewhere in Greece on an archaeological dig. I'm guessing the sun isn't even up there yet."

The sea slapped the sides of the boat as Alec set the inshore stern line. "Probably a summer rental."

"Brittany doesn't usually rent the cottage." Together they finished securing the boat, and Ryan winced as his shoulder protested.

Alec glanced at him. "Bad day?"

"No worse than usual." The pain reminded him he was alive and should make the most of every moment. A piece of his past that forced him to pay attention to the present. "I'll go over to the cottage in the morning and check it out."

"Or you could mind your own business."

Ryan shrugged. "Small island. I like to know what's going on."

"You can't help yourself, can you?"

"Just being friendly."

"You're like Brittany, always digging."

"Except she digs in the past, and I dig in the present. Are you in a rush to get back to sanding planks of wood or do you want a beer?"

"I could force one down if you're paying."

"You should be the one paying. You're the rich Brit."

"That was before my divorce. And you're the one who owns a bar."

"I'm living the dream." Ryan paused to greet one of the sailing club coaches, glanced at the times for high and low tides scrawled on the whiteboard by the dockside and then walked with Alec up the ramp that led from the marina to the bar and restaurant. Despite the fact it was only early summer, it was alive with activity. Ryan absorbed the lights and the crowds, remembering how the old disused boatyard had looked three years earlier. "So, how is the book going? It's unlike you to stay in one place this long. Those muscles will waste away if you spend too much time staring at computer screens and flicking through dusty books. You're looking puny."

"Puny?" Alec rolled powerful shoulders. "Do I need to remind you who stepped in to help you finish off the Ocean Club when your shoulder was bothering you? And I spent last summer building a replica Viking ship in Denmark and then sailing it to Scotland, which involved more rowing hours than I want to remember. So you can keep your judgmental comments about dusty books to yourself."

"You do know you're sounding defensive? Like I said. Puny." Ryan's phone beeped, and he pulled it out of his pocket and checked the text. "Interesting."

"If you're waiting for me to ask, you'll wait forever."

"It's Brittany. She's loaned Castaway Cottage to a friend in trouble, which explains the lights. She wants me to watch over her."

"You?" Alec doubled up with soundless laughter. "That's like giving a lamb to a wolf and saying 'Don't eat this'"

"Thank you. And who says she's a lamb? If the friend is anything like Brittany, she might be a wolf, too. I still have a scar where Brittany shot me in the butt with one of her arrows two summers ago."

"I thought she had perfect aim. She missed her target?"

"No. I *was* her target." Ryan texted a reply.

"You're telling her you have better things to do than baby-sit the friend."

"I'm telling her I'll do it. How hard can it be? I drop by, offer a shoulder to cry on, comfort her—"

"—take advantage of a vulnerable woman."

"No, because I don't want to be shot in the butt a second time."

"Why don't you say no?"

"Because I owe Brit, and this is payback." He thought about their history and felt a twinge of guilt. "She's calling it in."

Alec shook his head. "Again, I'm not asking."

"Good." Pocketing the phone, Ryan took the steps to the club two at a time. "So again, how's your book going? Have you reached the exciting part? Anyone died yet?"

"I'm writing a naval history of the American Revolution. Plenty of people die."

"Any sex in it?"

"Of course. They regularly stopped in the middle of a battle to have sex with each other." Alec stepped to one side as a group of women approached, arm in arm. "I'm flying back to London next week, so you're going to have to find a new drinking partner."

"Business or pleasure?"

"Both. I need to pay a visit to the Caird Library in Greenwich."

"Why would anyone need to go *there*?"

"It has the most extensive maritime archive in the world."

One of the women glanced at Alec idly and then stopped, her eyes widening. "I know you." She gave a delighted smile. "You're the *Shipwreck Hunter*. I've watched every series you've made, and I have the latest one on pre-order. This is *so* cool. The crazy thing is, history was my least favorite subject in school, but you actually manage to make it sexy. Loads of us follow you on Twitter, not that you'd notice us because I know you have, like, one hundred thousand followers."

Alec answered politely, and when they finally walked away, Ryan slapped him on the shoulder.

"Hey, that should be your tag line. *I make history sexy.*"

"Do you want to end up in the water?"

"Do you seriously have a hundred thousand followers? I guess that's what happens when you kayak half-naked through the Amazon jungle. Someone saw your anaconda."

Alec rolled his eyes. "Remind me why I spend time with you?"

"I own a bar. And on top of that, I keep you grounded and protect you from the droves of adoring females. So—you were telling me you're flying across the ocean to visit a library." Ryan walked through the bar, exchanging greetings as he went. "What's the pleasure part of the trip?"

"The library is the pleasure. Business is my ex-wife."

"Ouch. I'm beginning to see why a library might look like a party."

"It will happen to you one day."

"Never. To be divorced you have to be married, and I was inoculated against that at an early age. A white picket fence can look a lot like a prison when you're trapped behind it."

"You looked after your siblings. That's different."

"Trust me, there is no better lesson in contraception to a thirteen-year-old boy than looking after his four-year-old sister."

"If you've avoided all ties, why are you back home on the island where you grew up?"

Because he'd stared death in the face and crawled back home to heal.

"I'm here through choice, not obligation. And that choice was driven by lobster and the three-and-a-half-thousand miles of coastline. I can leave anytime it suits me."

"I promise not to repeat that to your sister."

"Good. Because if there is one thing scarier than an ex-wife, it's having a sister who teaches first grade. What is it about teachers? They perfect a look that can freeze bad behavior at a thousand paces." Ryan picked a table that looked over the water. Even though it was dark, he liked knowing it was close by. He reached for a menu and raised his brows as Tom, the barman, walked past with two large cocktails complete with sparklers. "Do you want one of those?"

"No, thanks. I prefer my drinks unadorned. Fireworks remind me of my marriage, and umbrellas remind me of the weather in London." Alec braced himself as a young woman bounced across the bar, blond hair flying, but this time it was Ryan who was the focus of attention.

She kissed him soundly on both cheeks. "Good to see you. Today was amazing. We saw seals. Will you be at the lobster bake?"

They exchanged light banter until her friends at the bar called her over, and she vanished in a cloud of fresh, lemony-scented perfume.

Alec stirred. "Who was that?"

"Her name is Anna Gibson. When she isn't helping out as a deckhand on the *Alice Rose*, she's working as an intern for the puffin conservation project. Why? Are you interested?" Ryan gestured to Tom behind the bar.

"I haven't finished paying off the last woman yet, and anyway, I'm not the one she was smiling at. From the way she was looking at you, I'd say she's setting her sat nav for the end of the rainbow. Never forget that the end of the rainbow leads to marriage, and marriage is the first step to divorce."

"We've established that I'm the last person who needs that lecture." Ryan slung his jacket over the back of the chair.

"So, what's a girl like that doing so far from civilization?"

"Apart from the fact that the *Alice Rose* is one of the most beautiful schooners in the whole of Maine? She probably heard the rumor that only real men can survive here." Ryan stretched out his legs. "And do I need to remind you that my marina has full hookups including phone, electricity, water, cable and Wi-Fi? I'm introducing civilization to Puffin Island."

"Most people come to a place like this to avoid those things. Including me."

"You're wrong. They like the illusion of escaping, but not the reality. The commercial world being what it is, they need to be able to stay in touch. If they can't, they'll go elsewhere, and this island can't afford to let them go elsewhere. That's my business model. We get them here, we charm them, we give them Wi-Fi."

"There's more to life than Wi-Fi, and there's a lot to be said for not being able to receive emails."

"Just because you receive them doesn't mean you have to reply. That's why spam filters were invented." Ryan glanced up as Tom delivered a couple of beers. He pushed one across the table to Alec. "Unless this is too civilized for you?"

"There are written records of beer being used by the Ancient Egyptians."

"Which proves man has always had his priorities right."

"And talking of priorities, this place is busy." Alec reached for the beer. "So you don't miss your old life? You're not bored, living in one place?"

Ryan's old life was something he tried not to think about.

The ache in his shoulder had faded to a dull throb, but other wounds, darker and deeper, would never heal. And perhaps that was a good thing. It reminded him to drag the most from every moment. "I'm here to stay. It's my civic duty to drag Puffin Island into the twenty-first century."

"Mommy, Mommy."

The next morning, devoured by the dream, Emily rolled over and buried her face in the pillow. The scent was unfamiliar, and through her half-open eyes she saw a strange pattern of tiny roses woven into white linen. This wasn't her bed. Her bed linen was crisp, contemporary and plain. This was like falling asleep with her face in a garden.

Through the fog of slumber she could hear a child's voice calling, but she knew it wasn't calling her, because she wasn't anyone's mommy. She would never be anyone's mommy. She'd made that decision a long time ago when her heart had been ripped from her chest.

"Aunt Emily?" The voice was closer this time. In the same room. And it was real. "There's a man at the door."

Not a dream.

It was like being woken by a shower of icy water.

Emily was out of bed in a flash, heart pounding. It was only when she went to pull on a robe that she realized she'd fallen asleep on top of the bed in her clothes, something she'd never done in her life before. She'd been afraid to sleep. Too over-whelmed by the responsibility to take her eyes off the child even for a moment. She'd lain on top of the bed and kept both doors open so that she'd hear any sounds; but at some point exhaustion had clearly defeated anxiety and she'd slept. As a result, her pristine black pants were no longer pristine, her business-like shirt was creased, and her hair had escaped from its restraining clip.

But it wasn't her appearance that worried her.

"A man?" She slid her feet into her shoes, comfortable flats purchased to negotiate street and subway. "Did he see you? Is he on his own or are there lots of them?"

"I saw him from my bedroom. It isn't the man with the camera." The little girl's eyes were wide and frightened, and Emily felt a flash of guilt. She was meant to be calm and dependable. A parent figure, not a walking ball of hysteria.

She stared down at green eyes and innocence. At golden hair, tumbled and curling like a fairy-tale princess.

Get me out of here.

"It won't be him. He doesn't know we're here. Everything is going to be fine." She recited the words without feeling them and tried not to remember that if everything were fine they wouldn't be here. "Hide in the bedroom. I'll handle it."

"Why do I have to hide?"

"Because I need to see who it is." They'd caught the last ferry from the mainland and arrived late. The cottage was on the far side of the island, nestled on the edge of Shell Bay. A beach hideaway. A haven from the pressures of life. Except that in her case she'd brought the pressures with her.

No one should know they were here.

She contemplated peeping out of the window, through those filmy romantic curtains that had no place in a life as practical as hers, but decided that would raise suspicions.

Grabbing her phone and preparing herself to draw blood if necessary, Emily dragged open the heavy door of the cottage and immediately smelled the sea. The salty freshness of the air knocked her off balance, as did her first glimpse of their visitor.

To describe him as striking would have been an understatement. She recognized the type immediately. His masculinity was welded deep into his DNA, his strength and physical appeal part of nature's master plan to ensure the earth remained populated. The running shoes, black sweat pants and soft T-shirt proclaimed him as the outdoor type, capable of dealing with whatever physical challenge the elements presented, but she knew it wouldn't have made a difference if he were naked or dressed in a killer suit. The clothing didn't change the facts. And the facts were that he was the sort of man who could tempt a sensible woman to do stupid things.

His gaze swept over her in an unapologetically male appraisal, and she found herself thinking about Neil, who believed strongly that men should cultivate their feminine side.

This man didn't have a feminine side.

He stood in the doorway, all pumped muscle and hard strength, dominating her with both his height and the width of his shoulders. His jaw was dark with stubble and his throat gleamed with the healthy sweat of physical exertion.

Not even under the threat of torture would Neil have presented himself in public without shaving.

A strange sensation spread over her skin and burrowed deep in her body.

"Is something wrong?" She could have answered her own question.

There was plenty wrong, and that was without even beginning to interpret her physical reaction.

A stranger was standing at her door only a few hours after she'd arrived, which could surely only mean one thing.

They'd found her.

She'd been warned about the press. Journalists were like rain on a roof. They found every crack, every weakness. But how had they done it so quickly? The authorities and the lawyers handling Lana's affairs had assured her that no one knew of her existence. The plan had been to keep it quiet and hope the story died.

"I was about to ask you the same question." His voice was a low, deep drawl, perfectly matched to the man. "You have a look of panic on your face. Things are mostly slow around here. We don't see much panic on Puffin Island."

He was a local?

Not in a million years would she have expected a man like him to be satisfied with life on a rural island. Despite the casual clothes there was an air of sophistication about him that suggested a life experience that extended well beyond the Maine coast.

His hair was dark and ruffled by the wind, and his eyes were sharply intelligent. He watched her for a moment, as if making up his mind about something, before his gaze shifted over her shoulder. Instinctively she closed the door slightly, blocking his view, hoping Juliet stayed out of sight.

If she hadn't felt so sick she would have laughed.

Was she really going to live like this?

She was the sober, sensible one. This was the sort of drama she would have expected from Lana.

"You live here?" she asked.

"Does that surprise you?"

It did, but she reminded herself that all that mattered was that he wasn't one of the media pack. He couldn't be. Apart from an island newsletter and a few closed Facebook groups, there was no media on Puffin Island.

Emily decided she was jumpy because of the briefing she'd had from Lana's lawyers. She was seeing journalists in her sleep. She was forgetting there were normal people out there. People whose job wasn't to delve into the business of others.

"I wasn't expecting visitors. But I appreciate you checking on us. Me. I mean me." She could see from the faint narrowing of those eyes that her slip hadn't gone unnoticed, and she wondered if he'd seen the little girl peeping from the window. "It's a lovely island."

"It is. Which makes me wonder why you're viewing it around a half-closed door. Unless you're Red Riding Hood." The amusement in his eyes was unsettling.

Looking at that wide, sensual mouth, she had no doubt he could be a wolf when it suited him. In fact, she was willing to bet that if you laid down the hearts he'd broken end-to-end across the bay, you'd be able to walk the fourteen miles to the mainland without getting your feet wet.

"Tell me what's wrong."

His question confirmed that she didn't share Lana's acting ability.

His gaze lingered on hers, and her heart rate jumped another level. She reminded herself that a stressed out ex-management consultant who could freeze water without the help of an electrical appliance was unlikely to be to his taste.

"There's nothing wrong."

"Are you sure? Because I can slay a dragon if that would help."

The warmth and the humor shook her more than the lazy, speculative look.

"This cottage is isolated, and I wasn't expecting visitors,

that's all. I have a cautious nature." Especially since she'd inherited her half sister's child.

"Brittany asked me to check on you. She didn't tell you?"

"You're a friend of Brittany's?" That knowledge added intimacy to a situation that should have had none. Now, instead of being strangers, they were connected. She wondered why Brittany would have made that request, and then remembered the panicky message she'd left on her friend's voice mail the night before. She obviously hadn't wasted a moment before calling in help.

Her heart lurched and then settled because she knew Brittany would never expose her secret. If she'd involved this man, then it was because she trusted him.

"We both grew up here. She was at school with one of my sisters. They used to spend their summers at Camp Puffin—sailing, kayaking and roasting marshmallows."

It sounded both blissful and alien. She tried to imagine a childhood that had included summer camp.

"It was kind of you to drop by. I'll let Brittany know you called and fulfilled your duty."

His smile was slow and sexy. "Believe me, duty has never looked so good."

Something about the way he said it stirred her senses, as did his wholly appreciative glance. Brief but thorough enough to give her the feeling he could have confirmed every one of her measurements if pressed to do so.

It surprised her.

Men usually found her unapproachable. Neil had once accused her of being like the polar ice cap without the global warming.

"If I married you I'd spend my whole life shivering and wearing thermal underwear."

He thought her problem lay in her inability to show emotion.

To Emily it wasn't a problem. It was an active decision. Love terrified her. It terrified her so much she'd decided at an early age that she'd rather live without it than put herself through the pain. She couldn't understand why people craved it. She now lived a safe protected life. A life in which she could exist secure in the knowledge that no one was going to explode a bomb inside her heart.

She didn't want the things most people wanted.

Flustered by the look in his eyes, she pushed her hair back from her face in a self-conscious gesture. "I'm sure you have a million things you could be doing with your day. I'm also sure babysitting isn't on your list of desirable activities."

"I'll have you know I'm an accomplished babysitter. Tell me how you know Brittany. College friend? You don't look like an archaeologist." He had the innate self-confidence of someone who had never met a situation he couldn't handle, and now he was handling *her*, teasing out information she didn't want to give.

"Yes, we met in college."

"So, how is she doing?"

"She didn't tell you that when she called to ask you to babysit?"

"It was a text, and, no, she didn't tell me anything. Is she still digging in Corfu?"

"Crete." Emily's mouth felt dry. "She's in Western Crete." There was something about those hooded dark eyes that encouraged a woman to part with confidences. "So you've known Brittany all your life?"

"I rescued her from a fight when she was in first grade. She'd brought a piece of Kathleen's sea glass into school for show-and-tell and some kid stole it. She exploded like a human firecracker. I'm willing to bet they could see the sparks as far south as Port Elizabeth."

It sounded so much like Brittany, she didn't bother questioning the veracity of his story.

Relaxing slightly, she took a deep breath and saw his gaze drop fleetingly to her chest.

Brittany had once teased her that God had taken six inches off her height and added it to her breasts. Given the choice, Emily would have chosen height.

"You knew Kathleen?"

"Yeah, I knew Kathleen. Does that mean you're going to open the door to me?" His voice was husky and amused. "Puffin Island is a close community. Islanders don't just know each other, we rely on each other. Especially in winter after the summer tourists have gone. A place like this brings people together. Added to that, Kathleen was a close friend of my grandmother."

"You have a grandmother?" She tried to imagine him being young and vulnerable, and failed.

"I do. She's a fine woman who hasn't given up hope of curing me of my wicked ways. So, how long are you staying?" His question caught her off guard. It made her realize how unprepared she was. She had no story. No explanation for her presence.

"I haven't decided. Look Mr.—"

"Ryan Cooper." He stepped forward and held out his hand, giving her no choice but to take it.

Warm strong fingers closed around hers, and she felt something shoot through her. The intense sexual charge was new to her, but that didn't mean she didn't recognize it for what it was. It shimmered in the air, spread along her skin and sank into her bones. She imagined those hands on her body and that mouth on hers. Unsettled, she snatched her hand away, but the low hum of awareness remained. It was as if touching him had triggered something she had no idea how to switch off.

Shaken by a connection she hadn't expected, she stepped back. "I'm sure Brittany will appreciate you dropping by to check on the cottage, but as you can see, everything is fine, so—"

"I wasn't checking on the cottage. I was checking on you. I'm guessing Eleanor. Or maybe, Alison." He stood without budging an inch, legs spread. It was obvious he wasn't going to move until he was ready. "Rebecca?"

"What?"

"Your name. Puffin Island is a friendly place. Around here the name is the first thing we learn about someone. Then we go deeper."

Her breath caught. Was that sexual innuendo? Something in that dark, velvety voice made her think it might have been, except that she didn't need to look in the mirror to know that a man like him was unlikely to waste time on someone like her. He was the type who liked his women thawed, not deep-frozen. "I don't think I'll be seeing much of people."

"You won't be able to help it. It's a small island. You'll need to shop, eat and play, and doing those things will mean meeting people. Stay for a winter, and you'll really learn the meaning of community. There's nothing like enduring hurricane-force winds and smothering fog to bring you close to your neighbors. If you're going to be living here, you'll have to get used to it."

She couldn't get used to it. She was responsible for the safety of a child, and no matter how much she doubted she was up to the task, she took that responsibility seriously.

"Mr. Cooper—"

"Ryan. Maybe your mother ignored the traditional and went for something more exotic. Amber? Arabella?"

Should she give him a false name? But what was the point of that if he already knew Brittany so well? She was out of her depth. Her life was about order, and suddenly all around her was chaos. Instead of being safe and predictable, the future suddenly seemed filled with deep holes just waiting to swallow her.

And now she didn't only have herself to worry about.

"Emily," she said finally. "I'm Emily."

"Emily." He said it slowly and then gave a smile that seemed to elevate the temperature of the air by a couple of degrees. "Welcome to Puffin Island."

CHAPTER TWO

SECRETS AND FEAR. He'd sensed both the moment she'd opened the door, just enough for conversation but not enough for the gesture to be construed as welcome.

He knew when a person had something to hide.

It was in his nature to want to unwrap secrets and take a closer look. He'd tried to switch that side of himself off, but still the instinct to ask questions, to dig and delve, persisted.

There were days when it drove him crazy.

To distract himself, he thought about the woman.

He'd woken her. One glance had told him she was the type who liked to be prepared for everything, and his visit had caught her unprepared. A few strands of silky hair had escaped from the clip on the back of her head and floated around smooth cheeks flushed from sleep. She'd been deliciously flustered, those green eyes focused on him with fierce suspicion.

She'd looked as if she were ready to defend someone or something.

Maybe that body.

Holy hell.

Ryan was proud that he hadn't swallowed his tongue or stammered. He'd even managed to keep his eyes on her face. Most

of the time. Then she'd taken a deep breath that had challenged
the buttons on her sober shirt, and those full breasts had risen
up as if hopeful of escape. The resulting jolt of sexual hunger
had been powerful enough to make him lose the thread of the
conversation.

It had been a struggle to keep his mouth from dropping open.
Even more of a struggle not to press her back against the wall
and prove that, even though they had Wi-Fi, not everything on
Puffin Island was civilized.

If he was lucky, she hadn't guessed how shallow he was.

Picking up the pace, he ran back along the coastal trail,
dropped down to the rocky shoreline and then climbed up again,
pushing hard until his lungs screamed for air and his muscles
ached. No one looking at him now would be able to guess that
four years earlier he'd died in a pool of his own blood. It was
thanks to the skill of medics he hadn't stayed dead.

He paused at the top because one of the promises he'd made
to himself was to take time to appreciate being alive. Of all
the places he'd traveled in his life he considered Penobscot
Bay, Maine, to be the most beautiful. Forty miles long and ten
miles wide, it stretched from Rockland on the western shore up
around the Blue Hill peninsula to Mount Desert. The scenery
ranged from wave-soaked rocky islands to lush national park.
To a waterman it was heaven, to an outdoorsman a playground.
To him, it was home.

On a day like today he wondered why it had taken him so
long to come back. Why he'd had to hit the bottom before making that decision. He'd stared into the mouth of hell and might
have fallen, had it not been for this place.

He'd swapped stress for sandy shores and rocky tidal pools,
the smells and sounds of foreign cities for the crash of the sea
and the call of the gulls, food he couldn't identify and didn't
have time to eat for lobster bakes and hand-cranked ice cream.
Instead of chasing the truth, he chased the wind and the tides.

He was smart enough to appreciate the irony of the situation. As a teenager he'd been so desperate to escape he'd fantasized about swimming the bay in the dead of night to get the hell off this island. He'd been trapped, imprisoned by circumstances, his cell mate the heavy burden of responsibility that had clung to him since the death of his parents. To keep himself sane, he'd dreamed about other places and other lands. Most of all he'd dreamed about being anonymous, of living in a place where the only thing people knew about you was what you chose to show them.

Taking a mouthful of water from the bottle in his hand, he watched a schooner glide across the bay, its sails plump with the wind.

On impulse, he pulled his phone out of his pocket and called Brittany. By his calculations it should be afternoon in Greece.

She answered immediately. "You're calling to tell me you messed with my friend?"

"I offered the hand of friendship as requested." He waited a beat. "You didn't tell me there was a child."

"It slipped my memory."

Knowing that nothing slipped her memory, Ryan wondered why she'd chosen not to tell him. "I was starting to think you'd done me a favor. I might have known there would be a catch."

"A kid isn't a catch. You treat children like viruses, Ryan. Man up."

He smiled. "So what's the story? You said she was in trouble. Am I to expect a visit from an abusive ex-husband?"

"Why does it matter? You'd handle him with one hand behind your back."

"I like to know what I'm dealing with, that's all."

"You're dealing with my stressed friend. Keep her safe."

Ryan thought about the fierce look in her eyes. "She's not exactly embracing my offer of help."

"No, she wouldn't." There was a pause. "Let's just say it wouldn't hurt for her to have another layer of protection."

"It would be helpful to know what I'm protecting her from."

"She'll tell you that when she's ready." The line crackled, and in the background he could hear Brittany having a conversation with someone called Spyros.

"Who is Spyros? Are you planning on marrying a Greek man and moving to Crete permanently?"

"I'm not marrying anyone. Been there, done that." Her flippant tone didn't fool him. He knew how deeply she'd been hurt in the past.

"Listen, Brit—"

"I have to go. I'll talk to you soon, Ryan." She broke the connection and he stared out to sea.

People fascinated him. The choices they made and the stories that lay behind those choices.

He knew Brittany's story. He wanted to know Emily's, and he thought about it now, his mind sifting through possible scenarios as he watched the waves rolling in.

He could have watched the ocean until the sun set, but he was needed back at the Ocean Club. They had to drain every drop out of the summer business to see them through the long Maine winter. He'd plowed all his money into the business and he was determined to make it pay, and not just because living here required him to earn money.

The island had given to him, and now he was giving back.

He had people depending on him.

Driving would have saved time, but choosing to live on this island had been about saving his sanity, not saving time, so he ran instead.

He ran down to the waterfront, past the old fisherman's cottage where Alec was no doubt absorbed in his research, and then took a shortcut inland.

The scent of the sea mingled with the smell of freshly mown grass and spring flowers.

This was his favorite time of year, before the flood of summer visitors swelled the population of the island, clogging roads and spreading across the beaches in a sprawl of people and picnic baskets.

Tourism poured welcome funds into the island's economy, but still there were moments when he resented the intrusion. It was like having guests in your home, and even welcome guests came with an expiration date.

Alec teased him that he couldn't give up those links to civilization—high-speed internet, phone signal—and it was true, but that didn't alter the fact that his choice to move here had been driven by a desire to change his life.

He wondered what had brought Emily to this place. There had to be a reason. There was always a reason.

She had a city look about her. Pale and pinched.

On Puffin Island doors swung open for visitors.

Hers had almost closed in his face.

He took a detour to the school, ran in through the gates and pressed the buzzer. "It's Ryan."

The door opened, and he strode through the cheerful foyer, past walls lined with brightly colored artwork.

His sister bounced out of the classroom, a vision of curls and color. Her dress sense had always been eclectic, and today she'd chosen an eye-popping combination of red and purple. She claimed that color made her happy, but Ryan knew she just had a happy disposition. She saw light where others saw dark and found exciting possibilities in small, daily tasks that to others appeared boring.

If he'd had to pick the perfect teacher for first graders, he would have picked Rachel.

Looking at her, he thought that maybe, just maybe, he hadn't entirely screwed up her childhood.

"Something wrong?" The concern in her eyes made him wonder when his family was going to stop worrying about him.

He was used to being the one in the role of protector, and the reversal made him uncomfortable. Presumably this was the price he paid for frightening them to death.

"Can't a man drop in to say hello to his baby sister? Why does something have to be wrong?"

"Because school starts in less than thirty minutes, you're sweaty and you only ever come and see me when you want something or you want to lecture me."

"That's harsh."

"It's true. And if you call me your 'baby sister' again, something *will* be wrong."

He looked at those bouncy curls and remembered spending impatient minutes trying to drag a hairbrush through the tangles when she was young. On more than one occasion he'd had to choose between dealing with the hair and being late for school, so he'd given up and bunched it back in a ribbon. It was lucky for him the kids at school hadn't known about his stock of ribbons.

Eventually she'd learned to do it for herself, but not before he'd learned far more than he ever wanted to know about braids and bows and girls' hair.

"You *are* my baby sister. And you still look as if you should be sitting in class, not teaching it."

She gave him the stare she used to silence overexcited children. "Not funny, Ryan. It was even less funny when you made the same joke last week when I was on a date with Jared Peters."

"I wanted to shake him up a little. The guy has a reputation."

"That's why I'm dating him."

Ryan reined in the urge to seek out Jared Peters and make sure he couldn't walk to his next date with Rachel. "That guy is all about having a good time and nothing else."

"Oh, please, and you're not?"

"He's too old for you."

"He's the same age as you."

"That's what I mean."

"Is there some reason I shouldn't have a good time as well or is this a 'man only' thing? Last time I checked, women were allowed to have orgasms."

Ryan swore under his breath and ran his hand over his face.

"I can't believe you used that word in this classroom. You look so wholesome."

"I'm not going to dignify that with a response."

"I'm looking out for you." For some reason an image of Emily's anxious face was wedged in his brain. She'd looked wholesome, too. And out of her depth. "That's my job."

"When I was four years old, maybe, but I'm all grown up. Your job is to let me make my own choices and live my life the way I want to live it."

Ryan wondered how parents did it. Wondered how they stood back and let their kids walk slap into a big mistake without trying to cushion it. "I can still step into the parent role when I need to."

She grinned. "Okay, Daddy."

"Don't even joke about it."

"We both know that raising us, me in particular, was the equivalent of being injected with a lifelong contraceptive."

"It wasn't that bad." It had been exactly that bad, to the point where there had never been a time in his life when he hadn't carried condoms. "I care about you. I don't want to see you hurt."

"Do you think you have a monopoly on that feeling? Do you think I enjoyed seeing you leave for all those dangerous places? It killed me, Ryan. Every time you left I wanted to beg you not to go, and then when I got that phone call—" Her voice broke. "I thought I'd lost you."

"Hey—" He frowned, unsettled by the emotion in her voice. "I'm still here."

"I know. And I love you. But you don't get to tell me how to live my life any more than I get to tell you how to live yours. You're my brother, not my keeper."

He held up his hands. "You're right and I'm wrong. You want to date Jared, then go ahead." But he made a mental note to have a deep and meaningful conversation with Jared next time he saw him.

Not that he had anything against him. Jared was a skilled

boat builder who was also a paramedic. Because of the rural nature of the community, most of the emergency care provision came from trained volunteers, and they played a vital role in island life.

"I don't need your permission, Ryan." There was a glint in her eyes. "Do I interfere with your love life? Do I tell you it's time you stopped thinking a relationship is all about sex and settled down? No, I don't. I love you, and I believe that eventually you'll figure out for yourself what you really want."

He raised his eyebrows. "You think I don't know what I want?"

She gave him a pointed look. "I have no comment on the way you live your life."

"Point taken."

Relenting, she stood on tiptoe and hugged him. "I'm glad you're alive. I'm even glad you're living here, but I look out for myself."

She'd been demonstrative and affectionate as a toddler, and she hadn't changed. She held nothing back. She didn't guard herself or search for the truth behind the surface people presented. She took them at face value. She trusted. She gave love freely and asked for nothing in return.

It frightened the shit out of him.

"Just don't say 'I love you' to Jared. Those words either encourage a guy to take advantage, or they send him running."

"You mean send *you* running. Not all men are like you."

"Hey, I used to cut up your food and walk you to school. You can't blame me for being protective."

"I'm protective, too. How's your shoulder?"

"It's fine." Dismissing it, he glanced at the walls of her classroom, pasted with the colorful artwork. "There's a woman staying in Brittany's cottage. I wondered if you knew anything about her."

"Ah, so now we're getting to the reason for the visit. A

woman." There was a gleam of interest in her eyes. "Why would I know anything?"

"Because there's a child." Ryan thought about the little face he'd seen peeping around the filmy white curtains in the upstairs bedroom. Was the child the reason Emily hadn't opened the door fully? That didn't make sense to him. In his experience children made people eager to connect, especially when they were new to a place. "I thought maybe you had a new pupil starting."

"Not before summer. There's just two weeks of school left." Rachel turned away to finish preparing for her lesson. "Why would you be interested in a woman with a child? We both know you've had enough of child rearing, and yes, I might just feel a tiny bit guilty about that, given that I'm the reason you can't stand the thought of settling down and having kids."

"Not true."

"Yes, it is. You were stuck looking after three little kids when you were a teenager. You couldn't wait to get away."

"Not because I didn't love you."

"I know that. All I'm saying is that I'm the reason you run from the idea of settling down. When we lost Mom and Dad, you had to do the serious stuff without any of the fun, so now you're having the fun. It's part of the reason you used to keep your bag packed, so you could run at a moment's notice."

He looked at her, his sweet-natured sister who had been orphaned at such a young age. "Hey, I've been living here for four years. That's stability."

She placed a large sheet of paper on the center of each low table. "There are still times I wonder if one day I'm going to wake up and find you gone. Not that it would matter if that's what you wanted," she said quickly. "You paid your dues."

He discovered that guilt could feel like sandpaper on a raw wound. "I didn't 'pay' anything. I did what needed to be done and I was happy to do it." If you ignored all the times he hadn't been happy and had complained like hell at the world for putting him in that situation. "And I'm not going anywhere. How could I after all the effort you put into saving me? I owe you."

"No one owes anyone anything, Ryan. We're a family. We help each other when we're in trouble. That's what family does. You taught me that." She walked across the classroom and picked up a bucket of seashells.

Even as a very young child she'd loved everything about the sea.

He'd spent hours with her on the beach, hunting for sea glass and building castles out of sand.

Ryan had always envied her calm contentment, a direct contrast to his own restless energy and burning desire to escape.

"What are you doing with those?"

"We're making a collage using things we found from the seashore on our trip last week. I still don't understand why you'd be interested in a woman renting the cottage, especially if there's a child in tow." She added paints and glue to each table. "Why the mystery?"

The mystery was that she'd been scared.

"I'm curious."

She flicked him a look. "Curiosity killed the cat, Ryan."

"If you can't come up with something more original than that, then there is no hope for the younger generation."

But he understood the reason for the tension. She was worried this wouldn't be enough for him. That he'd wake up one morning and decide to go back to his old life.

Since she'd been the one to clear up the mess last time, he couldn't blame her for hoping that didn't happen.

"Miss Cooper?" A small voice came from the doorway, and Ryan turned to see the Butler twins, Summer and Harry, hovering with their mother. Lisa Butler had moved to Puffin Island the summer before and had taken over the ice cream parlor, Summer Scoop, near the harbor.

While his sister worked her magic on two excited children,

Ryan smiled at Lisa. "Gearing up for the summer rush? How is everything?"

"Everything is good." Her expression told him everything was far from good, and instantly he wanted to know why. He couldn't help himself. Some might have said it was his passion, but he knew it was closer to an addiction, this need to find the truth buried beneath the surface. He wanted to know who, what, why, when. In this case he suspected the "what" was the state of the business. After a harsh Maine winter when the mention of ice cream was a joke not a temptation, Summer Scoop had to be suffering. The business had been limping along for years before Lisa Butler had decided to sink her life savings into it.

"I'll leave you to mold young minds, Miss Cooper." He nodded to his sister. "Talk to you later."

And in the meantime he was going to find out more about the woman in Castaway Cottage.

"Has the man gone?"

"He's gone." But his face was still in her head. Remembering the encounter, Emily felt heat rush through her body. "I'm sorry he woke you."

"He didn't." Those pale green eyes were ringed by tiredness, and Juliet's long hair fell in tangled curls of gold past narrow shoulders.

Emily looked for signs of tears, but there were none.

The girl seemed remote. Self-contained.

That was good, wasn't it?

She tried to ignore the simmer of unease in her belly that told her it wasn't good.

"Was the bed uncomfortable?" Emily had tucked the girl up in Brittany's old room the night before, covered with the patchwork quilt.

"It was noisy."

"That's the sea. You can sleep in a different room tonight if you like."

"Can I sleep with you?"

Emily swallowed. "Sure."

The little girl stood, staring up at the shelf in the kitchen. "Why are there jewels in a jar?"

"It's sea glass." Emily reached and picked up the jar. "It washes up on the beach. Sometimes it gets trapped in the pebbles and rocks. Kathleen used to collect it. Every time she went to the beach she came back with her pockets stuffed. She liked the colors, the fact that each piece has its own story." Relieved to have something to take her mind of Ryan Cooper, Emily handed Juliet the jar and watched as the girl turned it in her hands, studying each piece of glass closely, absorbed by color and shape.

"It's like a rainbow in a bottle."

"Kathleen kept it by the window so it caught the sunlight. She called it treasure."

"Does she live here?"

"Not anymore. She died a few years ago." Emily wondered if she should have used a different choice of words. Maybe she should have talked vaguely about heaven and stars in the sky. "She left this cottage to my friend, and sometimes, when one of us has a problem, we come here."

"Do you have a problem?"

Looking down at the problem, Emily felt compassion mingle with panic.

She didn't know anything about children, but she knew how it felt to have something you loved snatched from you. She knew how it felt to learn, at a far too young age, that life was cruel and unpredictable. That it could take as quickly as it gave, and with no warning.

"No. There's no problem now that we're here."

"Was she your family?"

"Kathleen? No. She was my friend's grandmother, but she was like a grandmother to me, too." And then she remembered "grandmother" probably meant nothing to a child whose short life had been spent among people paid to care for her and keep her away from a prying world. "Sometimes the people who are closest to you aren't the ones you're related to."

Let's make a promise. When one of us is in trouble, the others help, no questions.

The little girl held the jar to her chest. "You're my family."

"That's right." Her stomach lurched. Panic rose like the sea at high tide, swamping the deep fissures created by a lifetime of insecurities. She didn't want that responsibility. She'd never wanted it. "Why don't we explore the house? It was dark when we arrived last night."

Nestled in the curve of Shell Bay, Castaway Cottage had ocean views from all the front rooms. It was easy to see why Kathleen had never wanted to leave, despite the relative isolation and the long winters. She'd made sure that whatever the weather, there was warmth in the house. Wooden beams and hardwood floors formed a backdrop for furniture carefully chosen to reflect a nautical theme. A striped wingbacked chair, a textured rug, framed photos of the seabirds that nested around the rocky coast.

Still holding the jar, Juliet went straight to the window and clambered onto a chair. "Can we go to the beach?"

Emily felt a pressure in her chest.

Soon, she'd have to work out how she was going to handle that inevitable request, but she didn't have the energy for it now. "We need to settle in first. I have to unload our cases and unpack."

"I'm hungry."

Emily, whose usual caffeine-infused breakfast came in the form of strong coffee, realized she hadn't given any thought to feeding the girl. "I packed a few things in the car, but this afternoon we're going to need to go to the harbor and pick up some food."

Which presented her with another problem.

"I was thinking—" They walked back into the kitchen, and

Emily opened cupboards, hunting for food that Brittany might have left on her last visit. "Juliet is a pretty name, but how would you feel about being called something else?"

"Juliet is from Shakespeare."

"I know, but—" *Everyone else knows, too.* "Do you have another name? I'm Emily Jane."

"I'm Juliet Elizabeth."

"Elizabeth. How about Lizzy? That's pretty."

"Why do I need a different name? So the men with cameras don't find me?"

Emily favored honesty and saw no reason to alter that approach in this instance. "Yes." She opened a cupboard and pulled out a bowl in a pretty shade of cornflower blue. "That's part of the reason. I don't want people asking you questions. It will be like a game."

"I used to play games with Mellie."

"Mellie?"

"She cooks. Sometimes she looks after me when Paula is in the bedroom kissing her boyfriend."

"P—what? Who is Paula?"

"She's one of my nannies."

One of them? Still, at least Lana had arranged child care, which was more than their mother ever had. "So Paula looked after you?"

"Yes. And sometimes we watched my mom on TV." Lizzy was still holding the jar clutched against her chest. "Paula says people take pictures because she was famous and beautiful."

"Yes, she was."

People will pay money to see my face. You'll never be as pretty as me, and that's why people don't love you.

She tried to wipe the memory from her mind. "No one will take pictures of you here. People are friendly."

That much was true. She, Skylar and Brittany had spent plenty of happy evenings laughing and drinking in the Shipwreck Inn, and Brittany was well-known and loved on the island. Too well known.

She tried to remember whether her friend had ever mentioned a Ryan Cooper.

She was certain she hadn't met him before.

His wasn't a face that was easy to forget.

That face was in her head as she pulled open cupboards, looking through tins and dried pasta that Brittany left as emergency food. She found cereal, tipped it into the bowl along with the milk she'd bought and settled the child at the table. "We'll finish unpacking and then explore the island." Unpacking wasn't going to take long. Should she be depressed that everything she valued from her old life had fit into two small suitcases? A few clothes and her precious first editions. "We can have lunch by the harbor. You can pick anything you like from the menu. It will be fun."

"Can I bring my bear?"

Emily looked at the battered bear and decided its chances of surviving the trip were slim. There was a rip in its neck, and it had lost an eye. "Why don't we leave him here? We don't want to lose him." Or parts of him.

"I want him to come."

Concerned that half the bear might fall into the harbor, Emily was tempted to argue, but she was more afraid of doing something that might destabilize an already fragile situation. "We'll take the bear."

"Can I wear my fairy wings?"

Because fairy wings weren't conspicuous at all. She closed her eyes and told herself that no one would be looking for the child of a Hollywood actress on an island off the coast of Maine. And if Skylar was right, then Lizzy wouldn't be the only six-year-old wearing fairy wings. "If that's what you want." She stiffened as the child slid off her chair and walked across to her.

A small hand slid into hers. "Will they find us?"

The feel of that hand made the pressure in her chest worsen.
"No." She croaked out the word. "We're safe here."

Or at least, she hoped they were.

Picking up her phone, she found Brittany's name in her contacts and sent a text.

Who is Ryan Cooper?

BECAUSE IT WAS still early in the summer, she managed to park near the harbor. The busy working waterfront was a popular spot for tourists keen to experience all Puffin Island had to offer. Lobster boats, the lifeblood of the local community, bobbed alongside yachts, and fishermen rubbed shoulders with locals, tourists and sailing enthusiasts. The ferry that connected the island to the mainland ran three times a day when weather permitted. John Harris, the harbormaster, had been in charge of the service for as long as anyone could remember, terrifying everyone with his white shock of hair and heavy eyebrows.

From a distance, Emily recognized Dave Brown, who had been lobstering the waters around Puffin Island for three decades. She remembered standing with her friends, watching as he'd brought in the catch of the day, standing a safe distance from the deep waters of the harbor while Brittany and Kathleen had bought fish straight from the boat. They'd cooked it fresh and eaten it in the garden with butter dripping down chins and eager fingers.

"Can I see the boats?" Curious, Lizzy wandered toward the edge of the harbor, and Emily grabbed her shoulder and hauled her back.

Her heart was thudding and her palms were clammy. Why had she parked by the harbor? She should have found a side street and stayed as far from the water as possible.

John Harris walked across to them, a frown turning his eyebrows into a single shaggy line. "Careful. The water is deep here."

While Emily waited for her heart to slow down, she kept a grip on Lizzy. Brittany had once confessed the harbormaster had terrified her as a child, and Emily and Skylar had laughed, both unable to imagine Brittany being terrified of anything.

Lizzy didn't seem to share that fear. She looked from him to the ferry that was just leaving the harbor. "Is that the same ferry we came on last night?"

"It's the same. *The Captain Hook*."

"Like in *Peter Pan*?"

John Harris studied the child. "It's named for Dan Hook who donated the money for a ferry service fifty years ago. Is this your first visit to Puffin Island?"

"They're Brittany's friends." The male voice came from behind her, and Emily turned to find Ryan standing there. He nodded to John. "Busy ferry this morning."

"Full load. We're adding an extra crossing from next week as the summer season heats up." The introduction seemed to soften John Harris's mood a little because he nodded to Lizzy. "So, you're staying in Castaway Cottage. Best view on the island. Be careful by the water." He strode off, and Ryan shook his head.

"Don't let him scare you. A kid fell in once, and he's been nervous ever since. Summer is a busy time for him. So, you found your way to the harbor and Main Street. This is the closest thing we have to civilization. Can I direct you anywhere?"

He'd showered and changed since their encounter earlier that morning. He wore a pair of light-colored trousers and a dark blue shirt with the sleeves rolled up to the elbows. The addition of tailoring did nothing to disguise his powerful build.

Skylar would have observed that he was well put together.

Brittany would have described him as "smoking hot."

Emily found him unsettling. Not because he was so sure of himself—she was used to confident men, so that wasn't the reason—and not even because of the unexpected scorch of sexual awareness, although that was new to her. No, what frightened her was that those dark eyes seemed to see right through the invisible aura Neil had claimed made her unapproachable.

It suited her to be unapproachable. "I appreciate your concern, Mr. Cooper—"

"Ryan."

"Ryan, but we're fine."

"I didn't know you had a daughter."

She didn't correct him. "She's very shy. We were just—"

"I'm Lizzy."

Emily sighed. Right now shyness would have been preferable.

She waited for Ryan to make polite noises and back away. She was sure a man like him lived an adult-only life, free from the responsibility of children. Surprising her, he dropped into a crouch. The movement molded the fabric of his trousers to his thighs and pulled his shirt tight over broad, muscular shoulders.

"Hi, Lizzy. Nice bear."

Everything about him told her that he was a man's man, a person who could have been dropped in the wilderness with nothing but a knife and survived. Nothing had prepared her for the ease with which he handled Lizzy.

Watching him simply intensified her own feelings of inadequacy.

He took the bear and made admiring noises, his hands gentle as he handled the damaged toy. "What's his name?"

Name?

Not in a million years would she have thought to ask if the bear had a name, but apparently it did.

"Andrew." Lizzy's reply was hesitant, but Ryan nodded, as if the name made perfect sense to him.

"So, how are you and Andrew liking Puffin Island?"

Emily was grateful that the bear couldn't talk; otherwise he'd no doubt be reporting the fact that so far he'd been well and truly ignored.

If there was a Stuffed Bear Protection League, she was about to be reported for neglect.

She watched as Ryan handed the bear back carefully, envying the ease with which he talked to the child. He didn't use baby talk, nor was he patronizing or condescending. He behaved as if Lizzy had something to say that he was interested in hearing. As if the answers she gave were important to him. Some of the tension in Lizzy's shoulders melted away.

"I like the boats."

Why did it have to be the boats that had caught her attention?

Emily wondered what had possessed her to think coming to the island would be a good idea. She should have picked Wyoming or another state with no coastline.

"I like boats, too." Ryan rose to his feet. "What's your favorite food?"

This time Lizzy didn't hesitate. "Waffles. And chocolate milk."

"That's a lucky thing, because I happen to know somewhere that sells the best waffles you have ever tasted. And it has tables overlooking the sea so you can watch the boats at the same time. It will be my treat."

"Thank you, but we're fine." Emily found herself staring at him. He was at least a head taller than her. The casual attire did nothing to diminish the overwhelming sense of presence.

"You don't like waffles and chocolate milk?" There was humor in his eyes and something else. A sexy, lazy gleam that flustered her. He was the sort of man who made most women lose their heads and throw caution away with their underwear.

Emily had never lost her head or her underwear. Relationships were something to be thought through, measured and calculated, like every other important decision in life. She'd never found that difficult. But nor had she ever met anyone who made her feel the way Ryan Cooper did.

She'd spent three years with Neil and not once had he left her with this sense of breathless awareness. When he'd walked into a room, her heart rate hadn't altered.

"I appreciate the offer, but Lizzy and I have things we need to do before we have lunch."

Lizzy clutched the bear to her chest. "I'd like waffles."

To please her niece, she had to sit at a table with a man who made her feel as if she was naked?

He smiled. "Seems to me that what you need to do most of all is relax. You look as if you're about to explode."

"I've been driving for two days, and—"

"So a cool drink on the deck is just what you need to help you unwind."

"I don't need to unwind."

His gaze slid over her face. "There is more tension in your spine than in the mast of that yacht over there."

"I appreciate your concern, but if I'm stressed, then it's because I don't appreciate being stalked, Mr. Cooper."

"Stalked?"

"It seems as if every time I turn around, you're standing there."

"Welcome to island living, Emily. Chances are you're going to be bumping into me several times a day. And then there's the fact I promised Brittany I'd keep an eye on you."

"I appreciate your concern, but I'm absolving you of that duty."

"She told me you might need someone you could trust. She asked me to watch out for you. So, here I am, watching out for you."

Emily met that lazy, interested gaze and decided no normal, sane woman would be foolish enough to put her trust in a man like him. You might as well hand over your heart and say "stomp on this."

"I appreciate the offer, but I don't need anyone to keep an eye on me." In fact, people keeping an eye on them was the last thing she needed.

She was all that stood between Lizzy and a media hungry for a story at any cost.

They reminded her of vultures, swooping down to strip the last pieces of flesh from a carcass.

Lana was dead.

Surely that should be enough for them. Why did they need to unpick her life? There had been a constant parade of stories in the press. A catalog of salacious details that one day Lizzy might read.

If Emily could have found a way of destroying all of it, she would have done so.

Ryan stepped closer, his voice low. "Tell me what the trouble is, and I'll fix it."

She wondered how it felt to be that confident. It didn't seem to occur to him that there might be something he couldn't fix.

"It isn't trouble as much as a change in circumstances. Brittany was exaggerating."

And she was going to kill her.

"She said you'd push me away."

She wasn't just going to kill her; she was going to kill her slowly. "It was wrong of her to put you in this position. I'm sure you're a busy man, so you should get on and do whatever it is you do, and I'll—" She'd what? Carry on messing up parenthood? "I'll be fine."

"I made her a promise. I keep my promises." He gave a disarming smile. "And on top of that, I'm scared of Brittany. Apart from the fact she's an expert in Bronze Age weaponry and has an unnerving fascination for re-creating daggers and arrowheads, I remember what happened when someone stole her sea glass. I don't want to be on the wrong side of her temper."

She eyed those broad, powerful shoulders, noticing that his biceps filled out the arms of his shirt. She was willing to bet there wasn't much that scared him.

"Aunt Emily?" Lizzy tugged at her hand. "I'm hungry."

She saw Ryan lift an eyebrow and knew he'd filed the information that she was an aunt, not a mother.

"We'll buy some food. You can choose the things you like."
Because she had no idea what the girl liked.

"Harbor Stores is the best place for that. And don't miss
the bakery next door. They sell the best cheesecake I've tasted
outside New York." He broke off as an elderly lady crossed the
street toward him. The face was lined and the hair was white,
but there was no missing the twinkle in her eyes.

"Ryan Cooper, the most eligible man on the island. I was
hoping I might bump into you."

"I was hoping the same thing." He was all charm as he
reached out and took her arm. "All ready for tonight, Hilda?"

"I might have a problem with transportation because the
doctor told Bill he shouldn't be driving for a few weeks." She
looked at him hopefully, and Ryan didn't disappoint.

"What time are you planning on leaving? Seven?"

"Perfect. Will you drop me home afterward?"

He laughed. "You think I'm in the habit of leaving my date
stranded?"

"You're a good boy, despite all the rumors." She patted his
arm. "I hear all sorts of stories about all-night parties at the
Ocean Club, but I try not to listen."

Boy? Startled, Emily looked at the stubble that darkened
Ryan's jaw and the lazy, sleepy eyes. She saw nothing of the
boy in him, only the man. She wondered what the rumors were.

Women, no doubt.

With a man who looked like that, it had to be women.

"You're talking about Daisy's twenty-first birthday party. It
didn't last all night, but it's true that the sun was coming up."

"I heard she was wrapped like seaweed around the Allen
boy."

"Is that right?" It was clear that if he knew, he wasn't telling.
"If anyone else needs a lift tonight, let me know."

Emily liked the fact he wasn't prepared to reveal someone
else's secrets.

As someone currently guarding a big secret, it reassured her.

Hilda glanced around and then stepped closer to him. "This month's book was a shocker. It was Agnes's choice."

He looked amused. "You don't surprise me. My grandmother enjoys shocking people."

"True. I still remember the time she hired a nude model for our drawing class." The woman's face wrinkled into a smile. "We had better attendance that night than any other night in the history of our group. We had to paper over the windows to stop people peeping through the glass. This book was a step up from that." She noticed Lizzy and lowered her voice. "There were naked people *and* spanking." She gave him a knowing look, and Ryan's eyes gleamed.

"Now I'm thinking I should join the group."

"You can't do that. No testosterone allowed."

That would rule out Ryan Cooper, Emily thought. He was surrounded by a force field of testosterone.

"This is Brittany's friend Emily," Ryan said easily. "She's staying at Castaway Cottage, and this is her niece, Lizzy."

Hilda studied Emily closely. "I remember you. You're one of Kathleen's girls. You used to spend the summer here. You and the pretty blonde girl."

Emily hadn't expected anyone to recognize her. "Skylar."

"Kathleen talked about the three of you all the time. 'Hilda,' she said, 'those three are as close as sisters. They'd do anything for each other.' You were the quiet one." Hilda transferred her attention to Lizzy. "You're going to love Puffin Island. You should take a boat trip to see the seals and the puffins. And don't forget to visit Summer Scoop. Best ice cream in Maine and all organic. What's your favorite flavor?"

Lizzy considered. "Chocolate."

Emily felt something stir inside her.

Everyone knew the right way to talk to a child except her. They were easy and natural, whereas she used the same tone she used when presenting to a board of directors.

Miserably aware that she was only a few hours in to a responsibility that was going to last a lifetime, she watched as Ryan helped Hilda back across the street. If they were going to escape, this would be the perfect time.

She could walk to the store and do what she'd planned to do, stock up the cottage.

"Aunt Emily?" Lizzy was clutching the bear so tightly it seemed unlikely the stitching would survive.

Emily looked at the white knuckles and the lost expression on the child's face.

She didn't know anything about fairy wings or teddy bears, but she knew this.

She crouched down in front of Lizzy. "It must feel strange for you, being here without your—" *cook, nanny, cleaner, mother?* "—the people you know around you. It's strange for me, too. It's a new life for both of us, and it's going to take a little while before it feels normal." She didn't admit how afraid she was that it would never feel normal for her. "We don't know each other very well yet, so I won't always know what you want unless you tell me. It's important that you know you can ask me anything. Talk to me about anything. And if there's anything you want, you just have to ask."

Lizzy looked at her for a long moment. "I want waffles and chocolate milk."

CHAPTER THREE

RYAN ORDERED AT the bar and exchanged a few words with Kirsti who ran the Ocean Club and had made herself indispensable in the short time she'd been with them.

"Who is she?" Kirsti passed the order through to the kitchen and then glanced across to the deck, where tables had views across the bay. "She's pretty. Not in an obvious way, but in an interesting way. A little too innocent-looking for you, but it's time you mended your wicked ways, so that could be good. I think she could be The One."

Kirsti was obsessed with finding The One. It drove some people crazy. It made Ryan smile.

"It's a big world out there. If there really was only one person for everyone, we'd all be single."

"You are single. And you're mixing up sex with relationships." She selected a tall blue glass from the shelf. "A common mistake, particularly among the male sex, and the reason so many partnerships fail. You don't only need someone who can rock your body, you need someone who can rock your mind."

Ryan was fairly sure Emily would be able to do both, but Kirsti didn't need encouragement, so he kept that thought to himself. "Sometimes sex *is* the relationship."

"With you, sex is *always* the relationship. I bet you slap a page of terms and conditions in front of every woman you date."

"I don't, but it's a good idea. I'll run it past my lawyer."

She gave him a reproving look. "You're not funny."

"I'm hilarious. You just don't share my sense of humor."

"Does anyone? But this is my point! You need someone who is going to hold your attention. Your eye might be caught by a double-D cup, but your cynical heart will be caught by something more complex."

He glanced across at Emily's eye-popping curves. "My attention is caught. There's just one thing wrong. One thing that makes me completely sure she's not The One."

"Don't tell me—the child." With a sigh, Kirsti whipped up chocolate milk, added a straw and put the glass on the tray. "What do you have against children?"

"Nothing. I like children. I just don't want to be responsible for one."

"A bit of responsibility would do you good. Who is she, anyway?"

He knew all about responsibility, the sort that made you sweat and kept you awake at night. But Kirsti wasn't an islander, so she wouldn't know the details of his past.

"Friend of Brittany's. She's staying in Castaway Cottage."

"I love that place. The garden is like something from a fairy tale." Her eyes narrowed. "I think you might marry her."

"Jesus, Kirsti, keep your voice down." He was torn between exasperation and amusement. "For all you know, she's already married."

"She isn't. And the child isn't hers."

"How can you possibly know that?"

"The way she behaves. She isn't comfortable. It's as if this whole thing is new to her, as if they barely know each other and she isn't quite sure what her role is."

Ryan thought about the text Brittany had sent.

She's in trouble.

He wanted to know what the trouble was.

"There's no such thing as The One. Love is like Russian roulette. You have no idea what the outcome is going to be."

"You're such a cynic. Why do I work for you?"

"Because I pay better than anyone else on Puffin Island, and I don't fire you when you try to run a dating business on the side." Having successfully diverted the conversation, he strolled toward Emily. Kirsti was right. She looked uncomfortable. No, he corrected himself. Not uncomfortable. Shellshocked. Dazed. Gazing at her, he had the sense she was on the verge of snapping.

He tried to avoid women with baggage, and he suspected she had more baggage than an airline.

The baggage that really put the brakes on his libido was sitting with her legs swinging, waiting for chocolate milk.

He wove his way through crowded tables, noticing with satisfaction that very few were empty. He'd settled them at a table overlooking the beach, knowing that the view was the best on the island. From here you could watch the boats sailing between the island and the mainland. If you were lucky, you caught the occasional glimpse of seals on the rocky headland in the distance. So far they'd had three proposals on this deck, and one sunset wedding.

Almost everyone he knew chose a seat facing the water. He'd had to mediate between couples arguing with other couples over the tables with the best waterfront view.

Emily sat with her back to the water and her eyes on Lizzy as if she were afraid she might disappear in front of her. It only took a glance to see she was fiercely protective.

Keep an eye on her, Brittany had said.

He intended to do just that. Not just because a friend had asked him to, or because it was part of island culture to watch out for each other, but because he wanted to know the story. Kirsti was right that Lizzy and Emily didn't have the easy relationship of people who knew each other, and yet Lizzy had called her "aunt."

He wondered where Lizzy's mother was.

Was there a family crisis and she was filling in?

"One chocolate milk, extra large, two of the best-tasting coffees you'll find anywhere and a plate of our homemade waffles. They look so good I want to sit down and eat them with you." Kirsti placed everything on the table with a flourish and the smile that guaranteed her large tips and endless inappropriate invitations. "Enjoy. If you need anything else, let me know."

"Nothing else for me, thank you." Emily sent her a grateful glance. She had the air of someone who was improvising madly, feeling her way in the dark with no idea what she was meant to do next.

The breeze lifted a strand of her hair and blew it across her face. And her face fascinated him. Her eyes were the same green as the child's, her mouth soft and full, hinting at a sensuality hidden behind the tailored clothes. His mind leaped ahead, and he imagined her hair tumbling loose after a night of crazy sex. Given a couple of hours and a babysitter, he was fairly sure he could do something about her tension. Disturbed by how badly he wanted to put that thought into action, he lifted his hand to brush the strand of hair away at the same time as she did, and their fingers tangled. Heat ripped through his body.

"Sorry." He murmured the word and let his hand drop, watching while she anchored the offending locks with slender fingers. It was a blur of rich caramel and sunshine gold. He wanted to toss that damn clip into the water where she wouldn't be able to find it.

Because he didn't trust himself not to do that, he turned his attention to the child. The waffles had gone, the only evidence of their existence a pale smear of maple syrup over the center of the plate. "How is your chocolate milk?"

Lizzy sat on the chair, legs dangling, as she watched the boats glide across the bay, their sails curved by the wind. She'd needed two hands to manage the tall glass, so she'd put the bear down on the seat next to her. "It was good, thank you." She was stiff and polite, and it occurred to him he'd never seen a more uncomfortable pair.

He remembered Rachel at the same age, lighthearted and playful. She, too, had refused to be separated from her favorite toy, only in her case, the toy had been a puffin and she'd had a habit of leaving it everywhere.

He'd chased around the island more times than he cared to remember hunting for that damn puffin. On one occasion Scott Rowland, the island fire chief, had delivered it to the house after someone in the library had found it and recognized it as belonging to Rachel. Anticipating the day the puffin would be found by a tourist, not a local, Ryan had persuaded his grandmother to buy a spare, and he'd hidden it in his room as a precaution. His closest friend, Zach, had found it when they'd been sprawled in his room one day playing video games. It had taken Ryan six months to live down the fact he'd had a stuffed puffin in his room. Every week when he'd played football there had been a puffin in his locker. He'd dragged his skateboard out of the garage one morning only to find someone had painted a puffin on it. That had been the summer Ryan had given up skateboarding and taken up basketball. For one whole semester, the team had adopted the puffin as their mascot. By the time Zach had gotten bored with the joke, Ryan had enough stuffed puffins to give Rachel a whole colony of the things.

He'd gone to bed at night dreaming of living somewhere that didn't have Puffin in the name.

"So, Brittany is in Greece." He kept the conversation neutral, avoiding any topics that were likely to make her jumpy. Since he didn't know what those were, he figured it was best to stick to talking about her friend. "I remember when she was ten years old, she was playing at being an archaeologist, and she dug a deep hole in Kathleen's garden. When Kathleen asked what had happened to her flowers, Brit told her it was what was underneath the soil that was important."

Emily reached for her coffee. "You knew Kathleen well?"

"Very well. There is a group of women on the island, including Hilda, who you met earlier, who have been friends forever. They grew up here, went to school together and then married and had their children around the same time. They've seen each other through triumph and tragedy. Island life fosters friendships. They were as close as family." He saw her expression change. "You don't believe friends can be like family?"

"Oh, yes." There was a faraway look in her eyes. "I do believe that. Sometimes they can be better than family."

So, her own family had let her down.

He filed that fact away. "Over the years their meetings changed. When they had young children, it was a toddler group, a way of getting out of the house and breaking up the Maine winter. When the children were older, they turned it into a hiking club for a short time, and there was one summer when they took up kayaking. In the winter there was yoga, art—that was when the episode of the nude life drawing happened—and right now it's a book group." After he'd left home he'd stopped reading for a while. He put it down to all the times he'd read *Green Eggs and Ham* to Rachel.

"Where do they meet?"

"They used to meet in each other's houses, but now that's too much work for one person to cope with, so I let them use one of our function rooms, and provide the food."

"You own this place?" Curious, she glanced around. "It's busy. You're obviously doing something right."

"Took a lot of effort to design something that satisfied everyone. We needed it to work for the community." And he'd needed it to work for him. "The buildings and the marina were already here, but we made improvements, increased the number of member moorings and guest moorings, offered boat maintenance and a valet service. The first thing I did was employ a club manager. We had this huge building that was basically unused, so I converted it into apartments and kept the top one for myself. Then we developed this place and called the whole thing the Ocean Club. I worked on the principle that people who have just spent time at sea are happy to crash at the first decent place they find. We're full most nights in the summer."

"You've lived here all your life?"

"No. Like most people, I moved away, just to check there wasn't anything better out there."

"And was there?"

He thought about what he'd seen. The life he'd led. His shoulder throbbed, and he forced himself to relax because tension made it worse. "It was different. I grew up on this island. My grandfather was a lobsterman. My father took a different route. He spent time in the merchant marine and then joined the crew of the schooner *Alice Rose*, sailing around the coast."

"I don't know anything about boats."

Ryan wondered once again what she was doing on this island, where sailing was the main preoccupation. "That's a schooner." He pointed, and she turned her head reluctantly, leaving him with the feeling that if she could have found somewhere else to look she would have done so. "See the two masts? Some have more, but two is common. They have shallower drafts, perfect for coastal waters, and the way they're rigged makes them easier to handle in the changing winds along the coast, so they need a smaller crew."

Lizzy craned her neck. "It looks like a pirate ship."

Remembering Rachel saying the same, Ryan smiled. "My father became captain. He taught seamanship and navigation and then decided the teamwork needed to sail the *Alice Rose* should be transferable to the corporate world, so he persuaded a few of the big companies in Boston to send their executives up here. The rest of the time he offered coastal cruises to tourists and twice a year he ran bird-watching trips around the islands.

He believed that the best way to see the sea, the islands and the wildlife was from the deck of the *Alice Rose*."

Lizzy put down her empty glass. She had a ring of chocolate milk around her lips, and the breeze had whipped color into her cheeks. "Was he a pirate?"

"No. The opposite. He was a pioneer of sustainable ecotourism, which basically means he loved nature and tried to make sure that everything he did helped the island. He donated part of his profits to local conservation projects, particularly the protection of the puffins."

"What's a puffin?"

"It's a seabird. They used to nest on these islands a long time ago. Conservation experts have been finding ways to bring them back."

"This is their home? That's why it's called Puffin Island?"

"Yes, although now the puffin colony is on Puffin Rock." He pointed to the small uninhabited island just visible in the distance. "They lay one egg a year, and young puffins usually return to breed on the same island where they hatched."

"That's fascinating." Emily glanced at him, curious, and he noticed the dark flecks in her green eyes. The dark smudges under those eyes told him that whatever her trouble was, it was keeping her awake. Presumably it was also affecting her appetite given that all she'd ordered was coffee.

"I guess they have a sort of homing instinct." He'd done the same, hadn't he? In the end he'd dragged himself back here, to the place where he'd been born.

Lizzy's eyes were huge. "Can we see them?"

"You can take a boat trip. Humans can't get too close because otherwise they scare the puffins. Where is home to you?"

"New York." It was Emily who spoke, and he noticed she glanced at Lizzy and gave a brief shake of her head. He wondered what the child would have said without that warning glance to silence her.

Without looking at him, Emily reached for a napkin and

carefully wiped the milk from Lizzy's mouth. It was a natural response, something he'd done himself when his sister was very young, but something about the way she did it made him think it was new to her.

"You said you met Brittany at college. What were you studying?"

"Applied math and economics. We had rooms next door to each other."

"You, Brittany and—" he searched for the name "—Skylar."

"You know Sky?"

"No. But I've heard Brittany talk about her.

"So did Brit fill her room with skulls and old coins she'd dug up from the ground?"

Her brief smile was cut off by the sudden burst of loud laughter from a group behind them. She turned her head quickly, and her gaze was caught by something. A glance became a stare, and whatever it was that had drawn her attention unsettled her because her face lost color. Her smile gone, she fumbled blindly for her bag and stood up. "We should go. Thank you for the drink."

Ryan rose, too, and caught her arm. "Why the rush?" Standing this close, he caught the scent of her hair, saw the unusual blend of colors up close and acknowledged that his interest in her stemmed from something deeper than the desire to keep a promise made to a friend.

There was a cool breeze, but all he could feel was heat, and the strength of the attraction almost rocked him off his feet.

Her mouth was right there, and he knew if it hadn't been for Lizzy he would have kissed her. Maybe she would have slapped his face, but he would have been willing to take that chance.

The few relationships he'd had since his return to the island had been brief. His choice. A marine biologist who had spent a summer working in the research lab at the north of the island, a nurse who came from the mainland to help out at the medical center occasionally. He didn't know if they'd hoped for more because he hadn't asked. He lived his life in the moment.

"We have things to do." There was panic in her voice. "Thank you for the waffles and chocolate milk." She kept her back to the group and kept the child in front of her, shielding her from a threat invisible to Ryan.

"Goodbye, Ryan." Without waiting for a reply, she took Lizzy's hand and hurried her out of the café, keeping her head down and not looking back.

"Good to meet you, too," he murmured to himself, quashing the urge to stride after her and protect her from whatever perceived threat had sent her running from the table.

Sudden illness? She'd certainly been pale enough; but she'd been just fine moments earlier, so her health couldn't be responsible for the sudden shift in her attitude.

Hunting for clues, he rewound events in his head and remembered that she'd looked over her shoulder.

A swift glance revealed nothing but a group of young people who were spending the summer at the marine center on the north side of the island. Linked to the university, the floating laboratory ensured a steady stream of customers for the Ocean Club. They were loud, enthusiastic, in love with life and harmless. And untidy. They'd strewn their belongings over the table and vacant chairs. Backpacks, water bottles, leaflets detailing boat trips, a scientific magazine and a newspaper. They were deeply involved in a discussion about ecosystem-based fisheries management. He knew that at least a couple of them had the right to use "Dr." in front of their names. They were absorbed and argumentative and passionate. Not one of them had glanced over at their table.

There was no visible reason to justify Emily's abrupt departure.

"So you scared her away." Kirsti was back, clearing the plates. "You must be losing your touch. Still, at least you have a reason to chase after her."

Ryan lifted an eyebrow. "I do?"

"Sure." Kirsti put down the loaded tray and picked up the

bear. "She's not going to want to be without this. Unless she has a spare. When I'm a mom, I'm going to buy spares of everything."

Ryan took the bear. "She'll be back for it when she realizes she left it."

"Or you could take it to her." Kirsti added an empty glass to the tray. "You shouldn't let The One get away. That bear is the equivalent of Cinderella's slipper. Except that you know it fits."

Ryan rolled his eyes. "I changed my mind. You're fired."

"You can't fire me. I make great coffee, and I never complain when we're busy. And it's my moral duty to make sure people don't choose the wrong partners. Talking of which, those two at the table by the door are totally wrong for each other. I might have to interfere." She strolled off carrying the tray, Cupid in disguise.

Still holding the bear, Ryan started to follow her but accidentally knocked the chair behind him.

A bag and the newspaper fell to the floor, and he stooped to retrieve both with a murmur of apology.

Without thinking, he scanned the headline, something about health care reforms.

Returning the newspaper to the chair, he was about to walk back to the bar when something else caught his eye.

Juliet, Juliet, wherefore art thou, Juliet?

It wasn't the misquote of Shakespeare that caught his attention, it was the picture beneath it.

The media was still focused on the plane crash that had killed actress Lana Fox and her much older lover. There had been endless speculation about the whereabouts of her little girl.

Ryan grabbed the newspaper and took a closer look at the photograph, and in that single moment he had the answers he'd been looking for.

He no longer needed to speculate as to why Emily had run. He didn't need to wonder why she'd almost closed the door in his face or even why someone who knew nothing about boats had come to Puffin Island.

He knew.

And he knew why the child looked familiar.

CHAPTER FOUR

"WE HAVE TO GO BACK." Lizzy refused to move from the front door. "I left Andrew."

"It's late, Lizzy. Almost time for bed. We can't go back now. I'll phone the Ocean Club and explain. They'll keep Andrew safe."

"Nooo. I can't sleep without him. Someone might take him."

Emily didn't think a battered bear with one eye missing and a slit throat would fit most people's idea of a dream toy, but she kept that thought to herself. She was too busy beating herself up for making such a basic mistake. How could she have left the bear? And why hadn't she noticed sooner? It proved what she already knew—that she was the wrong person for this task. "Most people don't take things that belong to other people." Hoping her faith in human nature wasn't misplaced, she fumbled for her phone. "I'm going to call and ask them to keep Andrew. We'll pick him up tomorrow." By then the newspaper would have been thrown away, hopefully by someone more interested in tidying it up than reading it.

If she was lucky, no one would make the connection, but the incident had shaken her.

All thoughts of leaving the island faded. She needed to hide away, and there was no better place for that than Castaway Cottage.

Lizzy's face crumpled. "I want Andrew."

Emily's hands shook on the phone. "I'm going to make the call right now. Remember that nice girl, Kirsti? We're going to ask her to take care of Andrew until tomorrow."

Lizzy didn't answer. Instead, she ran into the living room and flopped down on the sofa with her face turned away.

Emily couldn't help thinking a tantrum would have been easier to handle, but she was learning that Lizzy's way of handling stress was to lock herself away.

She was looking up the number for the Ocean Club when there was a knock at the door.

What now?

Had someone recognized them?

Was this the moment she'd been dreading?

Braced for defensive action, she opened the door. She'd call the police. She'd sneak away in the night. She'd—

Ryan stood there, the bear in his hands. "I thought you might be missing this. I would have brought it over sooner but we've been insanely busy."

Emily sagged against the door frame. She'd never been so pleased to see anyone in her life. "You're a lifesaver. She adores that bear." She took it from him, wondering how to clone the battered bear. "I should have been more careful." She felt like hugging him but decided hugging Ryan Cooper probably qualified as a dangerous sport.

"Don't be hard on yourself. When my sister was Lizzy's age she was always losing toys. And you left in a hurry."

"We had things to do." Relief was tempered by caution. "It was kind of you to drive over. I don't know how to thank you. You're obviously busy, so—"

"It calms down around this time. The lull before the storm. Can I come in?"

Only minutes earlier she'd been wishing she wasn't on her

own with this. Now she was wishing the bear's rescuer had been anyone but him.

She wanted to close the door on all that raw masculinity, but he'd brought the bear and saved her life. She couldn't be rude to him simply because he made her feel things she didn't have time to feel right now.

Reluctantly, she opened the door wider. "I'll give Lizzy the bear."

She found the little girl exactly where she'd left her, lying listlessly on the sofa, staring at the wall.

"Ryan brought Andrew back." Dropping to her knees in front of the sofa, Emily tucked the battered bear into Lizzy's arms. "I promise we'll never leave him again."

Lizzy squeezed the bear so tightly Emily was afraid it might lose its head permanently.

Ryan watched from the doorway. "I love a happy ending." He glanced around the living room. "It's been a while since I've been here. You have no idea how many offers Kathleen had for this piece of land."

"It doesn't surprise me. But Brittany will never sell." She stood up. "Can I fetch you a drink? We haven't had time to stock up properly yet, but I have juice or soda. Or coffee?"

He followed her into the kitchen and scanned the bags on the table she hadn't yet unpacked. "That's not going to keep you going for long."

"It will do for now." Pulling milk out of the bag, she stowed it in the fridge. She had a carton of eggs in her hand when he spoke.

"Emily, I know."

"Sorry?"

He glanced over his shoulder, checking Lizzy was still in the living room. "I know why you ran."

She forced herself to keep breathing. "I don't know what you mean."

"The world is speculating on the whereabouts of Juliet Fox,

six-year-old daughter of troubled Hollywood actress Lana Fox who died a month ago in a plane crash along with the man everyone assumes was one of her lovers. Rumor has it the child is staying with a friend or relative in an unknown location." '

The carton of eggs slipped from her fingers and crashed onto the floor, spreading the contents in a sticky mess. "You saw the newspaper."

"I was looking for a reason for your abrupt departure."

Trying to think through the panic, she sank onto the nearest chair, ignoring the puddle of eggs congealing on the floor. "I came here because I thought we'd be safe."

"Safe from what? I assume you're her guardian."

"Yes, although as you can see, I'm not the right person for the job." She gripped her knees until her knuckles were white, and Ryan dropped to his haunches in front of her so they were eye level.

"Why aren't you the right person?"

"Do you want a list? First, I lose the bear, then, I risk exposing her by taking her out in public. I shouldn't have said yes to the drink." There was another reason why she knew she wasn't the right person, the most important reason of all, but that wasn't something she intended to share.

"I was the one who invited you for a drink."

"The responsibility was mine. You didn't know."

His eyes were dark velvet, his voice calm. "Are you seriously planning to hide away?"

"What choice do I have? I don't want the press to know we're here." She took a deep breath and tried to steady herself. "I talked to a bunch of people who have been with her since the accident. Lawyers, case workers, grief counselors. *My* head was spinning, so goodness knows what hers was doing. But the message I took from it all was that she needs to live as normal a life as possible. No media attention. No cameras. It freaks her out. There were great packs of them outside the house. One of them even got inside and cornered her, trying to get information about her mother. He's the one that scared her the most. Can you believe someone would actually do that? She's six years old. Six. I have to protect her from that."

His expression unreadable, he rose to his feet. "They told you her life needs to be as normal as possible. Not going out isn't normal. A child can't live her life trapped in a house and neither can you."

"I think she used to spend a lot of time in her old house, although of course, it was more of a palace than a house, and she had everything she needed within those walls and staff."

"You think? So you don't know her that well?"

"I don't know her at all." She reasoned that he already knew the part that could hurt them, so revealing detail wouldn't make a difference.

"Whatever her old life was like, it's gone. She needs to rebuild a life. And it needs to be a normal life. She doesn't need staff, she needs security."

"That's why I've already decided that from now on I'm only leaving the cottage when we need food."

"I don't mean that sort of security. I mean the sort that comes from knowing there are people around you who care about you and have your back. You can't keep her hidden in the cottage, Emily. Both of you will go crazy. She's a kid. She needs to explore and play. She needs to meet other kids. And what about you? Are you going to spend the next twelve years shut away here with no adult company?"

"I'm planning the next twelve hours. I can't think further ahead than that." Twelve years? The thought made her want to hyperventilate. "I'm going to need to make trips into town. She's too young to be left alone and I don't have anyone here I can trust."

"Hey, let's take this a step at a time." He sat down in the chair opposite her. "This is why Brittany said you were panicking."

There was much more to her panic and feelings of inadequacy than her ability to keep Lizzy's identity a secret. Eventually, she knew, media attention would move to other things, other lives, but she'd still be the child's guardian, and she knew she wasn't equipped for that monumental task. "When I told her what happened, she suggested I use the cottage. Kathleen left it to Brittany because she wanted her to have somewhere that was hers, somewhere she could go when life was tough. On our last day together at college Brittany gave us both a key."

"You and Skylar?"

"Yes. She said Kathleen would have wanted it. We were moving to different sides of the country. In Brittany's case, to a different continent half the time. It was somewhere we could come if we ever needed it."

"And you needed it."

"It seemed like a perfect place to hide while I worked out what to do."

For Lizzy it was perfect. For her, it was a nightmare. The crash of the waves kept her awake, churning up memories like the ocean churned sand on the seabed.

"What's your connection to Lana Fox?"

Emily was filled with a ridiculous desire to lean on all that hard strength, an impulse that made no sense because she'd been taking care of herself since she was younger than Lizzy.

"She was my sister." She saw his expression shift from concern to surprise. "I hadn't seen Lana since I left to go to college, and I met her child for the first time three days ago. We have no relationship. Lizzy has lost her mother and everything familiar and all she has is me." Panic bubbled up inside her. "That isn't good."

"Yeah, that must feel like a hell of a responsibility to shoulder alone. Is someone contesting the guardianship? Another relative?"

"There are no other relatives."

"Do you know the identity of the father?"

"Lana never told anyone. I'm all she has." Saying it aloud made it seem all the more terrifying.

"I didn't know Lana Fox had a sister."

"Half sister. We had the same mother. Different fathers."
Nameless, faceless men whom her mother had taken home after
one of her nights of endless drinking.

"I saw mention of her mother once. She was an alcoholic—"
His voice tailed off as he saw her expression change. "I apolo-
gize. She was your mother, too."

"I'm not afraid of facts, and the facts were that my mother
used to sleep with men when she was drunk and then face the
consequences sober. She died a couple of years ago. Her liver
decided it had been to one party too many."

"I don't remember Lana Fox ever talking about her family
in the press."

"She reinvented herself. We didn't exactly have a fairy-tale
childhood."

"Some fairy tales are pretty bad." He stretched out his legs.
"That woman in *Cinderella* was a real bitch."

It lightened the atmosphere, and a laugh bubbled up from her
throat. "Yes. And then there was the queen in *Snow White*. She
was a classic case of narcissistic personality disorder."

"Cruella de Vil was a serial killer."

"—of Dalmatians."

"True, but she demonstrated the same psychotic tendencies
seen in other murderers. Lack of compassion and lack of re-
morse."

"Maybe my childhood was closer to a fairy tale than I
thought."

"Too many elements missing. For a start, you didn't find your
prince." He glanced at her left hand. "You're single."

"Whenever I saw him climbing up the tower to my bedroom
I gave him a push."

"Yeah? Just for my own interest and research, what was it
that put you off?"

"He was creepy."

"Right." His smile faded. "So you and Lana weren't close as children?"

"I was the ugly sister."

"Given how manifestly wrong that description is, I assume it was hers."

"It wasn't wrong. She was very beautiful." Emily thought about the reality of her childhood. "And, no, we weren't close. We were just people living under the same roof for a little while. It was a shock when they called me to say she'd named me guardian, but then I thought about it and realized there wasn't anyone else. It was a decision made out of necessity, not choice."

"Did she leave you a letter?"

"Nothing."

"So one minute you were living your life, a life in which you'd had no contact with your half sister since you were a teenager, and the next you were guardian to her child. That is a major life change. Were you working? What did you do with the math and economics you studied?"

"Up until last month I was a management consultant. I worked for Taylor Hammond in New York."

He looked impressed. "That's the big-time."

"They had a reorganization and there was no job for me in the new structure. I was interviewing for new jobs when I found out about Lizzy." She clenched her hands in her lap. "Skylar would make some observation about how that was an indication that this was meant to be. How one day I'll look back and be pleased this happened."

Ryan gave a low laugh. "Kirsti would probably say the same thing. She believes in fate. So, are you missing New York? You had a life there."

Emily wondered if what she'd had could really be described as a life. "I had a job and a boyfriend."

"So there *was* a prince. You pushed him down the tower with the others?"

"He jumped. He got a look at the princess, decided she didn't look like a good deal and got the hell out." It helped to make a joke of it. "He dumped me a month ago."

"Not very princely behavior. And that was before Lizzy was on the scene. So it wasn't because of the child?"

"No." She stared at the mess on the floor. "Not because of that."

"How long were you together?"

"Three years. Two of which we lived together."

"Life really has dealt you a hand." His gaze was steady. Sympathetic. "I just want you to know I'm here for rebound sex or revenge sex whenever you need it. Just say the word. Or just grab me and explain afterward, whatever works for you."

She wouldn't have thought it possible to want to laugh at that moment, but she did. "Did you really just say that?"

"I really did. Want to think about it?"

The crazy thing was she had thought about it. What woman wouldn't? Ryan Cooper was insanely attractive. If all you were looking for was a night you'd never forget, he'd be the perfect choice. "I'm trying to be a responsible parent figure. I've already lost the bear. I think being caught having sex on the kitchen table would be a major fail."

"Possibly. So, just to clarify—the only thing that's stopping you is that your niece is asleep in the living room?"

"I can't believe I'm laughing. What is there to laugh about?"

"In my experience laughing always helps. So, what's your plan?"

"I got myself here. So far, that's it. I need to lie low while I work out what is best for Lizzy."

"And what about you?"

Her mouth was dry. "What about me?"

"You didn't sign on for this. It wasn't your choice." Something about the way he said it made her wonder if there was more to his comment than an astute observation.

"It wasn't a choice for either of us."

"I presume you chose the name 'Lizzy' because you're worried Juliet might draw attention."

"It's not a common name, and right now it's in the press a lot, so I thought it safer not to use it."

"Good decision. While the story is hot, the fewer people who make the connection, the better."

"But you know." As the implications of that struck her, she had to force herself to breathe. "What are you going to do with the information? The media would pay good money for a photo of Lana's child."

"Do I look like I need to sell a story to the media?" His mild tone coated layers of steel, and she squirmed because it seemed an uncharitable accusation, given he'd been nothing but helpful.

"I'm sorry. That was inexcusable. But I don't know you. And I don't know her, either."

"You know she likes chocolate milk and waffles."

She gave a wan smile. "Small steps."

He stood up. "Life is made of small steps. Let's start by clearing up the eggs before you slip. Breaking both your legs and knocking yourself unconscious isn't going to make the future easier."

"The eggs were for tomorrow's breakfast."

"I'll bring you breakfast. I'll be around at nine. Don't leave the cottage until I get here. That's the next twelve hours sorted. After that, we'll plan the next twelve hours. You can get through a life like that." With an efficiency that surprised her, he cleaned up the mess and stowed the contents of the bags while Emily went to check on Lizzy.

She found her asleep, still clutching Andrew.

"She's exhausted. I should put her to bed."

"I'll carry her upstairs." Ryan was behind her, and she shook her head.

"I can do it."

"Are you sure?" He eyed her frame. "You don't look strong enough."

"Careful. You're starting to sound like a fairy-tale prince. Just for the record, I'm capable of storming my own castle." She scooped Lizzy up in her arms and headed upstairs. She weighed more than Emily had expected, but she would rather have sprained her back than admit it to Ryan Cooper.

She lowered Lizzy to the bed, pulled off the little girl's shoes, tucked Andrew next to her and covered child and bear with the quilt. Then she stood, looking down at the feathery lashes brushing pale cheeks, and felt overwhelmed by the responsibility.

This wasn't temporary. This wasn't just for a few days or even the summer.

This was forever.

Subduing the panic, she stepped away from the bed. She couldn't think about forever.

She returned to the kitchen to find Ryan opening cupboards. "What are you looking for?"

"Wine?" He paused. "Or maybe you don't drink."

She knew he was thinking of her mother. "I drink. But I stop. Unfortunately wine wasn't one of the things I grabbed in my two-minute raid of Harbor Stores."

"Will coffee keep you awake?"

"I don't sleep, anyway." She was afraid to close her eyes in case something happened.

And now she had Lizzy in the bed with her.

"So, which is the worst part of all this? The boyfriend, the job or the kid?" He reached for a coffeepot while she found two mugs and put them down on the counter.

"Definitely the child."

"Not the boyfriend?"

"It would have ended eventually."

"Commitment phobia?"

"In a way."

"Plenty of men suffer from the same affliction."

"I was talking about me. I end all my relationships."

He gave her a curious look. "I would never have cast you in the role of serial heartbreaker."

"I try and disguise it. I sand the bedpost to hide the notches."

"So, what do you want out of a relationship?"

She watched as he moved around the kitchen and poured coffee into the two mugs, handing one to her. He looked competent and relaxed. "I don't want a traditional happy ending if that's what you're asking. Two children and a dog have never interested me."

"Which bit of that scenario bothers you most? The dog?"

She knew he was teasing, but this time she couldn't smile. "All of it bothers me."

"But you've ended up with a child, anyway."

"Yes." She walked to the window, trying to steady herself. "My favorite part of this house is the garden. We used to pick blueberries and eat them for breakfast."

"The climate and the soil are perfect here. You should try the blueberry ice cream at Summer Scoop on the harbor. It's delicious." Ryan paused. "What will you do about a job? Puffin Island isn't exactly a hub of activity for management consultancy firms."

"I'm not thinking about that right now." She sipped her coffee, thinking how strange it was having a man in her kitchen. "I'm still adjusting to being responsible for a child. I have some money saved up. I'll worry about the rest of it later."

"Does your ex-boyfriend know what happened?"

"No."

His eyes narrowed. "Let me get this straight. You were together for three years, and he hasn't once checked to see how you're doing?"

"The only people who know are Brittany and Skylar. And the lawyers, obviously. Even Lana's staff weren't told, for obvious reasons, since at least one of them let a journalist into the house. Who does that? Who stalks a child?" She put the mug down and stared over the garden. "I'm not going to be able to keep it a secret, am I? This place is going to be crowded with tourists in the summer. Someone is going to recognize her."

"Not necessarily. You forget that they're not looking. This isn't Hollywood. People come here to spend time away from the busy crush of their lives. They come here for the coast and the sea air."

"One of the locals will say something, then. Her picture was on the front page of the newspaper. They shouldn't be allowed to do that."

"The community is very protective of its own."

"But I'm not a member of the community."

"You're Brittany's friend, living in Brittany's cottage. That makes you a local."

"All it takes is one person. One call to the press and suddenly the island is flooded with them, like ants finding sugar to feed on."

He finished his coffee. "You're safe here tonight. Tomorrow we'll formulate a plan."

She knew a plan wasn't going to change the basic facts.

Like it or not, she was responsible for a child.

HE DROVE HOME along the coast road, saw a light burning in Alec's house, considered stopping in and then decided he'd end up fielding questions he didn't want to answer.

He avoided the bustle of the bar and went straight to his apartment. The building that now housed the Ocean Club Apartments had originally been a boatyard. It had stood empty for over three decades, battered by storms and winter weather, which was why he'd managed to buy the land for a ridiculously low price. He'd seen potential where others hadn't.

It had been a labor of love converting it, but his reward had been a profitable rental business and a premium apartment he could have sold a hundred times over. It stretched the length of the building and had a large glass-fronted open-plan living space that was always flooded with light regardless of season or weather.

At night he liked to sprawl on one of the sofas and watch the sun melt into the sea. Tonight he made straight for the office area in the corner and flipped open his laptop.

He hit the power switch and grabbed a beer from the fridge while he waited for it to boot up. Sprawling in the chair, he thought about the woman.

Those green eyes had been the first thing he'd noticed about her when she'd opened the door to him that day, closely followed by those delicious curves that no amount of discreet clothing could conceal.

The fact she'd put her life on hold to care for her orphaned niece was laudable, but at the same time put her strictly out of bounds.

Ryan wasn't looking for that level of complexity or intimacy in his relationships.

He'd had his fill of parenthood at an age when most kids had barely discovered the meaning of sex.

Without the plea from Brittany asking him to check on her friend, he would have stayed the hell away from her, and now that he had the facts, he was starting to wish he had.

He understood her situation better than she could possibly have imagined, which made the power of the sexual connection an inconvenience he was determined to ignore.

A woman with a child was not part of his game plan, and the fact that the child wasn't biologically hers made no difference. White knight was a role he avoided, right along with women who made noises about weddings and settling down.

Juliet Fox.

Brittany obviously hadn't mentioned his past. If Emily had known the truth, she definitely would have closed the door in his face.

With a soft curse he turned to his laptop and hit a couple of keys.

He started by searching the internet. He knew where to look to get the information he needed, and once he'd found everything he could without going deeper he reached for his phone and made one call.

"Larry?"

"Hey, stranger."

He could imagine his old colleague and adversary hunched over his untidy desk with papers overflowing over every square inch of space. "Slow news day?"

"Why would you care about the news? I thought you'd retired, yacht boy."

"I have, but the paper I saw today was enough to send a person to sleep. Lana Fox on the front page. What's that about?"

"Why do you care? Not exactly your area of interest, and anyway, last time I heard, all you read was tide tables. Are you thinking of coming back to the real world?"

"No. I'm just curious."

"Curious is one step from coming out of retirement."

"I'm not retired. I changed direction." Ryan picked up his beer, blocked out images that still kept him awake at night and stared at the information on his computer screen. "Tell me what you know about her."

"Lana Fox? She's dead."

"Yeah, I got that part. I was hoping for a little more depth."

"Depth and Lana Fox aren't words that sit comfortably together. What do I know? Total wacko. How she managed to hold it together in front of a camera, no one knows. Rumor has it they were threatening to fire her from her last film because she lost so many days on set."

Ryan stretched out his legs and stared out to sea. "The paper mentioned a kid." A kid she'd left in the care of an aunt she'd never met.

"Why would you be interested in that?"

"Can't imagine Lana as a mother, that's all. Didn't seem the type."

"Well, she wasn't Mary Poppins, if that's what you're asking me. I think she forgot she had a kid except for the few occasions when it suited her to show her off to the cameras. If you ask me, that child was a publicity stunt. Maybe she wanted the attention. She certainly had everyone speculating about the father. Who knows? Maybe she was going to reveal it at some point. Use it in some way. Casting couch in reverse. Woman on top."

Ryan thought about what Emily had told him about Lizzy being scared of cameras and photographers.

Mind working, he watched the lights from a yacht winking in the darkness. "Any idea what happened to her?"

"The kid? That's a mystery. There was some talk of family, but I always thought Lana invented herself with some pixie dust and a fairy wand. No one has been able to find out details. There's probably a story there if anyone can be bothered to look."

Ryan thought about the child fast asleep just a couple of miles away.

"Doesn't sound like much of a story to me."

"Me neither, but that's because I prefer something more challenging than trapping first-graders. So, why all the questions? You're tired of lounging around with lobsters and want to come back to the bright lights of the city?"

"That won't be happening anytime soon."

"Are you bored with being a tycoon? You thinking of starting up a newspaper? The *Puffin Post*?" Larry laughed at his own joke. "The *Crab Chronicle*."

"You are hilarious."

"No, you're the one who is hilarious burying yourself in the freezing wastes of rural Maine when you could have been here at the sharp end. You don't have to travel if you've lost the taste for it. You could pick your job. That's what happens when you were the best of the best. Come back. Dust off that Pulitzer prize. Return to the dark side."

"No." Ryan watched as the lights of a boat blinked in the bay. "Those days are over."

"They'll never be over. You're a born journalist. You can't help yourself. You smell blood and you hunt. So, is something going on there? Is that nose of yours on the scent of something?"

Ryan thought about Juliet Fox. About how much the media would love to get their hands on that juicy piece of information.

He thought about how Emily would react if she found out what his career had been before he'd moved back to the island.

"No," he said slowly. "I don't have anything. I'm living in the freezing wastes of rural Maine, remember? Nothing ever happens here."

CHAPTER FIVE

EMILY ROSE TO sunshine and blue skies after another night where sleep had barely paid a visit. Switching on her phone, she found a voice mail from Skylar asking how she was.

Ryan Cooper's dark, handsome features swam into her vision. Last night her anxieties about being responsible for Lizzy had been punctuated by thoughts of the calm way he'd dealt with her mini meltdown.

Pushing those thoughts aside, she texted Skylar, doing okay, thanks. She knew better than to mention Ryan to her friend, an incurable romantic. She sent a similar message to Brittany, who had asked the same question in a text sent in the early hours, and then slid out of bed.

Lizzy was still asleep, so she took a quick shower in Kathleen's pretty bathroom. Afterward she secured her hair on top of her head and reached for another pair of black tailored pants that were the staple of her wardrobe.

Sooner or later she was going to have to do something about that. She didn't own clothes suitable for casual beach living.

It felt strange not to be living her life checking the time and syncing calendars.

In New York her working day would have started hours ago.

If she'd been in the office she would have been at her desk by six in the morning. If seeing clients, she would probably have been thirty-thousand feet up in the air flying between meetings. Her life had been a series of stays in faceless hotel rooms and endless work on projects that would never be remembered by anyone. There had been no time to stand still, and she realized that the furious pace of her life had stopped the past settling on her.

Neil had wanted her to slow down and invest in their relationship.

She'd had nothing to invest. Emotionally, she was bankrupt. She took nothing and had nothing to give. Which was presumably why she had felt nothing when he'd ended it.

Wondering how her carefully ordered life could have spun so wildly out of control, she walked downstairs, brewed coffee and unlocked the door to the garden. She stood, breathing in the aroma of good coffee, absorbing the warmth. Here, the sound of the birds almost drowned out the sound of the sea.

It was a sun trap, sheltered from the whip of the wind and designed as a sanctuary for nature. Kathleen had planted carefully, perennials clustered together in a haze of purples, blues and yellows to attract the bees. Wildflowers, moss and fern grew between rocks, and butterflies danced across petals dappled by sunlight.

It was a perfect peaceful spot. There had been summers when she'd spent hours curled up on one of the chairs reading, lost in worlds that weren't her own.

"Aunt Emily?"

She turned to see Lizzy standing there, eyes sleepy, her hands holding tightly around the bear.

"Hi." Emily softened her voice. "You slept?"

"Can we go to the beach?"

The fleeting calm left her. "Not today." Sooner or later she was going to have to face that challenge, but not yet. Braced for an argument, she was relieved to hear the sound of a car. "That will be Ryan. He's bringing breakfast."

"Waffles?"

"Let's find out." She should probably have been pushing healthy food, but she told herself there was plenty of time for that. Reluctantly she left the tumbling tranquility of the coastal garden and walked to the front door.

Ryan stood there, one large hand holding several bags stuffed with groceries, the other holding the lead of a thoroughly over-excited dog, a spaniel with eager eyes and soft floppy ears. "Sit. *Sit!* Do not run into the house. Do not jump up—" He broke off as the dog sprang at Emily and planted his paws on her thighs. "Sorry. I think you can see who is in charge." He dumped the bags on the porch, reached out and hauled the excited dog away from her, but Emily dropped to her knees, unable to resist those hopeful eyes and wagging tail.

"You're gorgeous." She crooned, talked nonsense, smoothed satiny soft fur with her hand and was rewarded with more affection than she could ever remember receiving in her life before. When the dog planted its paws on her lap and tried to lick her face, she put her hands on all that scrabbling warmth and laughed. "He's yours?"

"It's a she and, no, not mine. A dog is a responsibility, and I'm not interested in anything that dictates the way I live my life." But his hand was gentle as he removed the wriggling animal from Emily's lap. "Calm down. She doesn't recognize either of those words, by the way. Her vocabulary is a work in progress. So far *food* is the only word she's sure about."

"Who does she belong to?"

"My grandmother. Unfortunately she had her hip done last winter and hasn't fully recovered her mobility, so walking Cocoa is now my job. I try and delegate, but we're busy at the Ocean Club today, so she had to come with me. I thought she could play in the garden while we have breakfast."

A week ago she'd had neither dog nor child in her life. Now she had both. "We're keeping you from your work."

"My staff will thank you. They have more fun when I'm not there."

Taking advantage of his lapse in concentration, the dog darted into the cottage, paws sliding on the floor, and cannoned into Lizzy who was standing in the hallway holding her bear.

Unsure how Lizzy felt around dogs, Emily reached her in two strides and scooped her up. "Her name is Cocoa and she won't hurt you." The child was rigid in her arms, and she wondered if lifting her had been a mistake. Should she have lifted Cocoa instead? She was about to lower her when she felt those skinny arms slide around her neck and tighten. Silken curls brushed against her cheek, and she felt warm breath brush against her neck as Lizzy burrowed into her shoulder in an achingly familiar gesture. Something woke and stirred deep inside her, and Emily closed her eyes.

Not now.

This wasn't the time to start remembering.

"Is she all right?" Ryan made a grab for the dog. "You are a bundle of trouble. My grandmother thought a dog would keep her youthful, but this animal has put ten years on me."

Dragging her mind back to the present, Emily lowered Lizzy gently, and dog and child stared at one another.

The dog whined and lay down on her belly at the little girl's feet.

Ryan's eyebrows lifted. "I guess we know who wields the power. Nice work, Lizzy. She likes you. From now on, you're in charge. Put your hand out and let her sniff you."

The dog stood up, tail wagging, and thrust her damp nose into the child's palm.

Lizzy smiled. The first smile Emily had seen since she'd picked her up at the airport along with a suitcase. One suitcase, but more baggage than one small person should have to carry alone.

Emily licked dry lips. Right now it was her own baggage that was troubling her.

Grateful for the distraction provided by the dog, she retrieved the bags Ryan had abandoned on the step and carried them through to the kitchen.

He followed her. "You didn't sleep."

"How do you know that?"

"Pale face. Dark circles. It's a dead giveaway. Don't worry, I have the perfect gift for you." He dipped his hand into one of the bags and pulled out two tall cups stamped with the swirling logo of the Ocean Club. "Iced cappuccino with an extra shot made by Kirsti's fair hand."

Emily reached for the cup gratefully. "I might love you."

He grinned. "Don't threaten me so early in the morning." He sprawled in the nearest chair, coffee in his hand, the bags abandoned on the table. "So, you were awake all night wondering how many people saw that newspaper."

"Not just that. I'm used to city noises. I can't sleep here." She hadn't slept a full night since the phone call that had given her a child she wasn't qualified to raise.

"Most people find the sound of the sea soothing."

She wasn't most people. "What else is in the bags? Please, tell me it's a month's supply of iced cappuccino."

"Better. You said you didn't have time to stock up, so I thought I'd help. Here—" he pushed a bag toward her "—start with that one." He glanced over his shoulder as Lizzy came into the room with Cocoa. "What's your favorite color, Lizzy?"

"Pink."

"Then this is your lucky day." He pulled something pink from another bag and handed it to her. "It's a hat. I thought when you were out in town, you might like to wear it." His gaze flickered to Emily. "To keep the sun out of your eyes."

And prying eyes away from her face, Emily thought, as she loaded the fridge and cupboards. Smart thinking. She wished she'd thought of it herself.

"What would you have done if she'd said blue was her favorite color?"

Ryan dipped his hand back in the bag and produced a blue one.

Lizzy clutched the pink one possessively. "I like this one. What do the words say?"

"Do you recognize any of the letters?"

"The writing is curly." Lizzy stared hard and spelled out a few letters. "It says something *Cl-ub*."

"Ocean. It says Ocean Club." Ryan traced the words with his finger. "It's a very special hat. Only people who have eaten waffles on the terrace can have one."

Emily was touched. "Thank you. That was thoughtful."

His gaze connected briefly with hers, and she felt that same ripple of awareness she'd felt on the first day. For a moment she stood, mesmerized by the unapologetic interest in those dark eyes. She had no idea how to respond. Her relationship with Neil had been comfortable, her emotions and feelings around him safely predictable. He'd never threatened her heart rate or her equilibrium. Ryan threatened both, and he knew it.

He turned his attention back to Lizzy. "Keep the brim pulled low, and it will keep the sun off her face. Not that I think there's much risk of exposure."

Emily understood that the "exposure" he referred to wasn't solar driven.

Lizzy tugged it onto her head. "I like it."

"Do you know Cocoa's favorite game?" He dipped his hand into another bag and pulled out a ball. "Fetch. Take her into the garden and throw the ball. She'll bring it back to you."

Child, ball and dog tumbled into the garden to play while Emily stared dizzily at the image of her new life.

A month earlier she'd been living in Manhattan. Jobless, admittedly, but with plans and ambitions. At least two companies had made positive noises about employing her. When she'd thought about the future, it hadn't looked like this.

It was like booking a flight to Europe and finding yourself in the middle of the African desert, unprepared and unequipped.

"I didn't know she couldn't read fluently. I don't even know what age most children start to read."

"It varies. Rachel was reading by four. Others take longer, but as long as they get there in the end, I don't see why it matters."

"You know a lot about children." And she hadn't expected that. He seemed like the type of man who saw children as nothing more than an inconvenient by-product of sex. And then something occurred to her, something that made her stomach lurch. "Are you divorced? Married?"

"You think I left my wife in bed to come here and eat breakfast with you? You have a low expectation of relationships, Emily. And I'm not married." He looked at her in a way that made her heart beat faster and her insides melt, but what really worried her was the sudden and unexpected lift of her mood that came from the knowledge he was single.

Why should she care that he was single?

Her life was already complicated enough, and when she eventually got around to thinking about relationships again, it wouldn't be with a man like him.

"You're comfortable with young children. The sort of comfortable that usually comes from having them."

"So now you're asking if I spent my wild youth populating Maine?"

He was attractive and charming. She had little trouble believing he'd had a wild youth.

She watched as he unpacked the last of the bags. She was aware of every tiny detail of him, from the flex of shoulder muscle to the scar visible on the bronzed skin above his collarbone.

Feeling her scrutiny, he turned his head, and his gaze met hers. Slowly, he put the bag down, as if he could no longer remember why he was holding it.

Heat rushed through her, infusing her cheeks with livid color.

Oh, God, she was having sex thoughts about a man she barely even knew.

She felt as if she'd been caught watching porn.

"Did you ask me a question?" His voice was roughened, his eyes fixed on hers, and she knew he'd forgotten the conversation.

She'd forgotten it, too. "Sex. I mean, populating Maine," she stammered. "Children, yes, that was it. Children."

His gaze held hers steadily. "Children have never been on my wish list."

"So you don't have experience?"

"I have tons of experience."

"Nieces? Nephews?"

"Siblings. Three of them. All younger." He reached for the bottle of maple syrup he'd brought with him. "I was thirteen when my parents were killed. The twins, Sam and Helen, were nine, and Rachel was four. It was a typical Maine winter. Snow, ice and no power. They collided with a tree. It was all over before anyone could get to them." He spoke in a modulated tone that revealed all of the facts and none of the feelings.

She didn't know what she'd expected to hear, but it hadn't been that.

The story saddened her on so many levels. It proved that even happy families weren't immune to tragedy.

"I'm sorry."

"My grandmother moved in and took over parenting, but three kids were a challenge, and her health has never been good."

"Four." Emily put down the loaf of bread she'd unpacked. "You were a child, too."

"I left childhood behind the day my parents were killed." His face was expressionless. "I remember the police coming to the door and the look on my grandmother's face when she told me what had happened. The others were asleep, and we decided not to wake them. It was the worst night of my life."

She knew exactly how he would have felt because she'd felt it, too, that brutal loss of someone who was part of you. Like ripping away flesh and muscle down to the bone, the wound going so deep it never really healed. Eventually it closed over the surface, leaving bruises and scars invisible to the naked eye.

"How did you cope?"

"I don't know if you'd describe it as coping. I just got up every day and did what needed to be done. I helped get them up in the morning before I went to school and came home at lunchtime to give my grandmother some respite. Bedtime was fun. The twins slept in bed with my grandmother for months, which left me with Rachel. She clung to me like a monkey for the first two years after our parents were killed. In the end I dragged her bed into my room because I was getting no sleep, and my grades were dropping."

She studied those broad shoulders, her mind trying to construct the boy he was then from the man he was now. She imagined him cradling his little sister while struggling with his own loss. "Lizzy has been sleeping in the bed with me."

His glance flickered to hers. "Yeah, she probably feels safer that way. She's afraid you might disappear, too."

Emily didn't say that she felt like a fraud. Unworthy of the trust Lizzy had placed in her.

"But you had three siblings—so much for you to manage."

"We weren't on our own with it. The islanders pulled together. We didn't cook a meal for the first year. They set up a rotation, and every day something would appear. Things got easier once Rachel started school and the twins were teenagers. Thanks to our background, they were pretty independent, and there was always someone to turn to if they had problems."

He'd had a web of support. He'd suffered, but he hadn't been alone.

Her first experience of loss had been suffered alone.

Disturbed by her own feelings, she took her cappuccino to

the French doors that opened from the kitchen on to the pretty garden. Lizzy was chasing around the grass with the dog.

Not in a million years would she have thought to give Lizzy a pet. The grief counselor had advised her not to make any changes, to allow Lizzy time to adjust, but watching child and dog rolling around the garden simply proved there were no rules for handling grief. You did whatever helped you get through another day.

She turned and looked at Ryan. "Where are they now? Your siblings?"

"Rachel is a teacher at Puffin Elementary. She loves island life. Loves the water and loves kids. In the summer she works at Camp Puffin on the south of the island. She teaches kayaking. Sam is a doctor in Boston, and Helen works as a translator for the United Nations in New York. They turned out okay, considering all the mistakes I made." He said it with humor, but everything he told her somehow served to underpin her own sense of inadequacy.

"Did you read a lot of parenting books?"

"None. I relied on intuition and, as a result, screwed up repeatedly."

And yet it had been intuition that had driven him to return the bear and bring the dog for a visit, something she was sure would never have occurred to her. There had never been a place for animals in her life.

"Did you ever think you couldn't do it?" The words tumbled out, revealing more than she'd intended to reveal, and Ryan gave her a long, steady look.

"Is this about me or you?"

Her hand shook on the cup, and she put it on the nearest countertop. "Did you ever worry that you wouldn't be able to keep them safe?"

"Safe from what?"

"Everything." Her mouth felt as if she'd run a marathon through the desert. "There are dangers everywhere."

"I made plenty of mistakes, if that's what you're asking. Fortunately, kids are resilient. They survived the culinary disasters, the laundry mistakes, the fact I couldn't sew and didn't have a clue about child development. Rachel followed me everywhere. I think she was afraid I might disappear like our parents."

She tried to imagine it. The teenage boy and the little girl. "It must have been a wrench when you left to go to college."

"Are you kidding?" He gave a short laugh. "After spending my teenage years with three kids crawling all over me, I was so desperate to escape this place I would have swum to the mainland if that was the only way to leave the island. By then I had my bedroom back, but I was looking forward to a night that didn't start with reading *Green Eggs and Ham.*"

"You didn't miss them?"

It was a moment before he answered. "I loved them, but, no, I didn't miss them. I badly needed to get away and have a life that didn't include school plays and parent-teacher conferences. My grandmother had help from the other women in her group and several of the islanders. In a way, they were an extended family. They had rotations for babysitting, collecting from school. When there were school events, Rachel had all of them in the front row."

It made her smile. "This was the same group who were meeting for book club the other night?"

"Yeah. And Kathleen, of course."

"You had a great deal of responsibility at a young age. That's why you're not married?"

He laughed. "Let's just say I value my independence. The ability to come and go as I please. I don't plan on giving that up anytime soon."

Emily picked up her coffee, pulled out one of the pretty blue kitchen chairs and sat down. Through the open door she could see Lizzy throwing the ball over and over again while the dog bounded after it, tail wagging. "The first time I met Kathleen, I couldn't believe she was real. I'd never met anyone like her.

She was so kind and genuine and interested. She never expected anyone to conform. She truly valued individuality."

"Yes. She was a special woman with a gift for reading people."

"I barely spoke on my first visit." Emily took a sip of coffee. "I was overwhelmed by everything. The exchange of ideas. Laughter. It was alien to me because my home life was nothing like that."

If he was wondering how her home life was, he kept the questions to himself. "You came often?"

"Every summer. I had nowhere else to go, and Skylar would do just about anything to avoid going home, so Brittany invited us here."

"It wasn't enough to be together at college?"

Emily finished her coffee and put the cup down. "When Brittany invited me into her room on that first day, I wondered how on earth I'd survive living next to someone as volatile as her. Skylar arrived a couple of minutes later, dropped off by the family chauffeur rather than her parents because they thought she was throwing away her life studying art when she could have been a lawyer. I took one look at her clothes and assumed we'd have nothing in common. I admired her dress, trying to be polite, and she told me she'd made it herself for less than ten dollars. Then Brittany took a call from her lawyer about her divorce while we sat open-mouthed. I assume you know all about that as you're friends?"

He didn't look at her. "Yeah, I know."

"She was a mess, but in a way it broke the ice. Right from the start there were no barriers. We talked until we couldn't keep our eyes open. At the beginning, all we had in common was that we'd been let down by the people closest to us. Maybe it was a sense of isolation that brought us together. I don't know, but we understood each other. Our friendship grew from there."

"I can't believe our visits didn't overlap."

"Maybe we didn't notice each other." Her heart thudded uncomfortably as his gaze locked on hers.

"I would have noticed you."

"Ryan—"

"I would have noticed you." His voice was soft, his eyes fixed on her face with such unwavering attention that she felt something uncurl deep inside her.

Most people looked at another person and saw the surface. Ryan ignored the surface and looked deeper, as if he'd learned that the face someone presented to the world had no more substance than a picture.

He hadn't touched her, and yet her skin tingled and her body heated.

The tense, delicious silence was broken by Lizzy, who came back into the kitchen, the dog at her ankles. "Can she stay with us?"

With visible effort Ryan transferred his gaze from Emily to the child.

"I have to take her back to my grandmother, but I'll bring her to see you again soon." He leaned forward and picked up the final bag. "I've brought you some things to keep you busy." He pulled out a bucket and spade in bright sparkly pink. "You are living next to one of the best beaches on the island. You're going to want to make the most of that."

And just like that, the mood was shattered.

Emily stared at the bucket, numb, while Lizzy reached for it.

"Emily doesn't like the beach."

Pulling herself together, Emily stood up. "We've been busy, that's all. Maybe in a few days."

"I could go by myself."

"No. You mustn't go near the water." The words came out in a rush and she saw Ryan's eyes narrow. "I— We— Let's take a few more days to settle in and then we'll see. The bucket is a thoughtful gift, Ryan. And the hat was a great idea."

What wasn't a great idea was a trip to the beach.

She knew she wasn't ready for that.

She wasn't sure she ever would be.

Skylar arrived late Friday afternoon, bringing an explosion of color and city sophistication to their peaceful existence. "I've brought provisions." She winked at Emily, delved into the bag and pulled out a parcel that she handed to the child.

Lizzy looked at her, dazzled by the halo of golden hair and the bright smile. Skylar wore a cluster of silver bangles on her wrists, and they clinked together as she moved her arms. Lizzy lasted five minutes before climbing onto a chair to take a closer look.

"They're shiny."

"They're silver. Want to try one on?" Sky slid one off her arm. "I made them."

Lizzy was wide-eyed with awe. "How?"

"It's what I do. I make jewelry." She made it sound like a fun hobby, but Emily knew Skylar was starting to make ripples, not just in the jewelry world but also with her glass. She'd recently had a small exhibition in New York, showing not only glass and jewelry, but also ceramics and some of her artwork.

Lizzy fingered the bracelets. "Could I make them?"

"Yes. Not silver, but there are other types of jewelry that are just as pretty. We'll make something tomorrow. The first stage is always design. Do you have paper and coloring pens?"

Lizzy shook her head and Sky smiled. "Look in the white bag. There are glitter pens underneath the fairy wings and tiara."

Emily rolled her eyes. "Why not a cowboy outfit?"

"Wanting to be a fairy princess is a perfectly reasonable ambition when you're six." Skylar thrust a bulging bag toward her. "This is for you."

"You bought me fairy wings and a tiara?"

"I bought you the adult equivalent. Something suitable for a summer at the beach, so you don't have to walk around looking as if you're taking a lunch break from running a prison. You're welcome." Sky leaned forward and hugged her tightly. "Stop wearing black and undo a few buttons. Let the sunshine in. If you won't do it for me, do it for your health. Maine has over forty-five identified species of mosquitoes, and black just happens to be their favorite color. Right now you are an insect banquet."

Later, much later, after a supper of pizza and ice cream followed by a girlie movie marathon, they waited for Lizzy to fall asleep and then curled up on Kathleen's sofas and shared a bottle of wine.

"I'd give anything for a slice of Kathleen's apple-topped ginger cake." Skylar stretched her arms in a long, languid movement that reminded Emily of a contented cat. "With maple cream."

"It would cost you around a week pounding on the treadmill."

"It would be worth every stride and every bead of sweat."

"I don't know how you can keep such terrible eating habits and stay so slim."

"It's nervous energy. So, how has it been?" Settling into the sofa, Sky curled her legs under her, her waterfall of white-blond hair flowing over her shoulder. "I didn't see anyone with cameras when I arrived."

"No. I'm starting to think I overreacted. If they're looking, they're not looking here. Ryan thinks they'll be bored with it soon."

"Ryan? You met a man?" Skylar looked interested. "Tell me more."

"He's a local businessman. He owns the Ocean Club. Friend of Brittany's."

"Friend? Friend, as in someone she knows, or someone she's had sex with?"

"I haven't asked." And she wasn't sure she wanted to know the answer.

"That's the difference between us. It would have been my first question. Let's ask her, although I'm pretty sure she would have told us if there was something to tell." Sky reached for her phone. "Is he sexy?" She tapped at the keys and pressed Send.

Emily thought about the hard planes of his handsome face and the power of that body. *Oh, yes.* "Why is that relevant?"

"Because you need some light relief after Neil. You'll have lines on your forehead before your time, and no man should ever do that to a woman." Putting her phone down, Skylar leaned forward and topped up her wineglass. "Do you trust him?"

"Ryan? Yes." It surprised her to discover that she did. "Tell me about you. How is Richard?"

"Busy. Running for senate means he isn't home much. He wants me to give up my business and travel around the state with him. He says he needs my support." She talked quickly and Emily listened, dismissing the nagging voice in her head that told her Skylar wasn't suited to that life.

Who was she to give advice?

What did she know about long-term, functioning relationships?

"Do you want to give up your business?"

"No. I love what I'm doing and it's going well. A new store in Brooklyn has just agreed to stock my jewelry, and a gallery in London is hosting an exhibition for my new collection *Ocean Blue*, so I'm crazy busy getting ready for that."

"You have an exhibition in London? Skylar, that's wonderful!" Emily reached across and hugged her friend. "I'm so proud of you. Wow. Richard must be proud, too. And your parents? Surely now they can see this is right for you."

Skylar took another gulp of wine. "My choice of career is something my parents don't mention. And Richard doesn't want me to go to London."

"He doesn't—" Emily was thrown. "But this is *huge*. Why wouldn't he want you to go? He should be so proud of you."

"The timing is bad. If he wins in November, he'll want me by his side for all the Christmas functions." Skylar put her glass down, her eyes miserable. "And I hate the way things are right now, Em. I bump into my parents and it's as if we're strangers. The only thing I've ever done right in their eyes is date Richard Everson. They want me to go home to Long Island for the holidays."

"You said you weren't putting yourself through that again."

"I know what I said. They want me to bring Richard. And he wants to go, of course, because he needs my father's support. So I'm facing a miserable Christmas with my parents, being held up as an example of a daughter who wasted her life. My younger brother passed the bar exam by the way, so I'm now officially the only non-lawyer in the family." The smile stayed on her face, but her voice was thickened. "Whatever happened to the fairy-tale Christmas we used to dream about, Em? What happened to ice-skating, roasting chestnuts and family fun? Christmas in my house is about as much fun as a day in the Supreme Court."

"You can't give up your exhibition, Sky. They should be excited for you! They should— On second thought, don't get me started on that one." Emily flopped back against the sofa. "Can you believe this? On the outside you have the perfect family, but you're no better off than I am."

"I know. My friendship with you and Brit has been stronger than anything I've had with my family." Sky stared down into her glass. "The other reason I don't want to go home for the holidays is that I'm afraid Richard is going to make some dramatic gesture."

"Like what?"

"I don't know. He's hinting at marriage again. He thinks it will help his image."

Emily almost spilled her wine. "He wants to marry you because he thinks it will garner him public approval? What about what you want? And, more to the point, what about love?"

"I asked that exact same question."

"And?"

Skylar took a mouthful of wine. "He told me not to be ridiculous. Said that of course he loves me. That goes without saying."

"Love should never go without saying." Emily felt a flicker of unease. "You did tell him how you feel about marriage?"

"Of course. I've always been honest about it. He knows it isn't what I want. For me a relationship should be held together by strong emotions, not a piece of paper." Some of the sparkle in her eyes dimmed. "Do you think I'm too romantic?"

"For believing in love? No, but that isn't what matters. What matters is finding a man who understands and respects your views, whatever they are." And she was fairly sure Richard wasn't that person. Emily found his charm superficial and manipulative rather than genuine. She would never have put him with someone as creative and sensitive as Sky. It was like sending an armored tank to catch a butterfly. "Relationships are hard. Finding someone who wants the same things as you is rare. Finding someone who understands you, even rarer."

"Are you about to tell me you had that with Neil? Because I won't believe you."

What had she had with Neil? She wasn't sure she could put a name to it. "It was an easy relationship."

"Is easy another word for boring?"

"Maybe. It was safe. I was with him for three years and not once did I ever feel confused about my feelings." She'd known Ryan two days, and her feelings had been all over the place.

"It was your lucky day when he dumped you. The only thing I don't understand is why you didn't dump him first. You deserve so much better. All you need to do now is throw out everything black in your wardrobe."

"I like black."

"It makes you fade into the background."

"That's exactly where I want my body to be. In the background. You have no idea how many men have had conversations with my chest."

"And I bet you managed to get them to look into your eyes two seconds after you opened your mouth. You're bright and witty, Emily. Your body is your body. It's the only one you have, and you shouldn't feel you need to hide it."

"You don't understand. Even Neil agreed that my breasts, if not exactly my worst feature, were unfortunate."

"He said that? I'm glad you told me because now if I ever get the chance to kill him, I'm going to make sure it's a slow death. Why do you think he said that, Em? Because underneath the surface he was a jealous creep, and he didn't want other men looking at you."

Emily tried to picture Neil jealous. "I want people to take me seriously."

"I understand. Look at this blond hair—" Skylar lifted a handful of pale silk "—do you think people don't prejudge me? Of course they do, but I don't care. I love my hair, and if they want to take it as a sign that my brain is minuscule, then it will give me all the more pleasure to prove them wrong. This isn't about the way you relate to men. It's to do with your mother."

Emily examined her nails. "Maybe."

"Not maybe. She used her body because she had a pathological need for attention and didn't know any other way to get it. You're nothing like her."

"Sometimes when I look in the mirror, I see similarities."

"Change your mirror. I am going to take a pair of scissors to your clothes. It's time you stopped hiding. You deserve a grand passion, and your breasts deserve to have a life outside the rigid confines of corsetry."

Emily stared wistfully into her wineglass. "I've never had a grand passion. I've never felt that strongly about anyone. I'm not sure I want to."

"That's because you associate passion with the sleazy encounters your mother had. But that wasn't passion. That was opportunistic sex."

Emily thought about the constant parade of men when she was growing up. The cramped apartment had been busier than Times Square in July. The walls had been paper thin, the lack of air-conditioning adding to the oppressive atmosphere of the place. She was fairly sure her mother hadn't been a passion addict, just an attention addict. "Lana inherited some of her traits. She had that same desperate need to be the focus of attention."

She'd worked hard to be the opposite, but in doing so she'd put a label on passion as something to avoid, which had proven to be easy enough until now.

She thought about Ryan and the way he made her feel. Of the sexual awareness simmering beneath the surface of every interaction. "Do you see a future with Richard?"

Skylar lay back on the sofa. "He has many qualities that I admire. He knows what he wants and he's determined to do what he has to do to get there."

"And he wants you." She didn't voice her uneasy suspicion that Richard saw Skylar as an acquisition, a tool to enhance his political appeal.

"Yes, but there's no escaping the fact that we're different. He has a five-year plan. I have a five-minute plan."

"I love that about you."

Sky finished her wine and put her glass down, "How is it going with Lizzy?"

"It's tough. I feel like I want to tie her to me so that nothing bad can happen." Emily toyed with her glass. "I don't trust my ability to keep her safe. I don't have the skills for this."

"Yes, you do, but you're scared." Sky took her hand. "It's understandable after what happened. You're an intelligent woman, you should understand that."

"What I know intellectually doesn't change how I feel emotionally." She stared down at Skylar's slender fingers, relieved to be able to talk about it. "When I got that phone call, I thought Puffin Island was the perfect place to bring Lizzy. Secluded, miles away from her home, but I didn't think about the other things."

"You mean the sea?"

"Yes. I couldn't have brought her to a worse place. All my phobias are concentrated in this one small island."

"You love this island. We spent every summer here when we were in college."

"That was different. I didn't have a child to care for. I could think about myself. I helped Kathleen in the garden, I walked up through the woods, I spent time in the kitchen with her learning to bake—"

"So, you can still do those things." Skylar put her glass down. "You don't have to go to the beach, Em."

"It's right outside the door and she keeps asking." She took a deep breath. "And I feel like a coward."

"You're not a coward. You had a terrible experience. And you've only been back on the island for a week. Give yourself time. There's no shortage of things to do here. We just need to get her interested in things that don't involve the sea." Skylar suppressed a yawn. "I haven't been to the harbor for ages. We'll do that tomorrow. We'll eat ice cream and you can take me to the Ocean Club. I want to try the chocolate milk Lizzy keeps talking about. And I want to meet Ryan."

RYAN WAS SEATED at a table by the water talking to Alec when Kirsti strolled over to them.

"She's back. I told you she was The One. She can't stay away from you. And she brought a hot blonde for Alec."

Alec didn't lift his gaze from the book he'd been reading before Ryan had joined him. "I'm allergic to hot blondes."

Ryan glanced over to the doorway, saw Emily and Lizzy and, behind them, another woman he assumed to be Skylar.

She was tall, her almost ethereal beauty emphasized by the dress she wore. A mixture of green and blue, it floated round her slim frame as she walked.

"She looks like a mermaid," Kirsti muttered. "Alec, you are going to want to look at this."

"In Greek mythology mermaids summon men to their doom."

"You read too much. You need to watch more TV and play some video games. Rot your brain a bit like normal folk."

Ryan's gaze was fixed on Emily. It had been two days since he'd seen her, and he'd had to force himself to stay away and give her space. He saw her smile at something her friend said and felt something clench in his gut. There, right there, was the real Emily. He wanted to capture that smile and follow it to see where it led, but it vanished quickly, and she was watching the child again, as if she were afraid she might blow away in the breeze. He understood that the responsibility was new to her, but he sensed there was more to her overly protective attitude than the unfamiliarity of unplanned parenthood. "Give them the same table as last time."

"It's reserved for the couple sailing that racing sloop. There will be pistols at dawn."

"I'll handle them. Give it to Emily."

"You're the boss." With a shrug Kirsti moved away to welcome her new customers.

Convenience should have made Emily take the seat with the best view of the water, but instead she switched with her friend so that she once again sat with her back to it.

Pondering the possible reasons for that, Ryan tried to focus on the conversation with Alec. "So, you're planning to see Selina while you're in London?"

Alec wrapped his hand around the beer. "Yes, but that's one encounter that will be as brief as possible."

"I don't understand how the two of you ever got together."

"Never underestimate the mind-distorting power of great sex." Alec stared broodingly over the ocean. "Before me, she dated bankers and mega-rich city types. She wanted adventure and thought I was a sea-loving version of Indiana Jones. I took her kayaking on our honeymoon."

Ryan raised his eyebrows. "White water kayaking?"

"No, just plain old sea kayaking. Her hair got wet. Let's talk about something else."

"I've got a better idea." Ryan stood up. "Put your book away. We're moving tables. You're going to talk to a live human instead of reading about dead ones."

"Dead ones are more interesting, and they don't bleed you dry. And I am not moving tables. I like this table. It seats two people which means no one can join us."

"I own this place," Ryan murmured. "If you don't move, I'll physically eject you."

With a sigh, Alec looked up. "Are you meddling with my sex life? Because I have enough of that from Kirsti."

"No. I'm meddling with my own, and you're my wingman."

"I'm not a good wingman."

"You're the perfect wingman. You're so bitter and twisted, you make me look good. Stand up. We're going to join them for lunch."

Alec's gaze flickered to Skylar, and just for a moment he stared. "Women like her don't eat lunch. They order it, make you pay and then push it round their plates."

"Every time you think like that, you're letting your ex-wife win."

"She has won. She has a large chunk of my income and my house in London."

"You have plenty of income left, you can stay in a hotel when you travel to London and you have your freedom. Seems like a good deal to me." Ryan gave him a slap on the shoulder and strolled across to the group on the other side of the terrace. Lizzy sat, swinging her legs, and she reminded him so much of Rachel at the same age, he smiled. "Cute hat."

Her face brightened. "Ryan! Can I play with Cocoa?"

"And there was I thinking you were pleased to see me, but it's all about the dog." He winked at her. "She's with my grandmother, but you can visit anytime. They live in the big white house with the wraparound deck just up from the harbor. If you wanted to walk Cocoa, you'd be her favorite person."

Lizzy instantly turned to Emily. "Can we?"

"Sure." Her gaze flickered to his, and he saw color warm her cheeks in the moment before she turned to introduce her friend. "This is Skylar."

He was tempted to ask Skylar if she'd babysit while he took Emily for a long walk along the beach followed by sunset-watching from the king-size bed in his apartment, but instead he reached across and extended his hand.

"I've heard about you from my grandmother." He took the chair next to Emily, leaving Alec no choice but to sit next to Skylar. "This is Alec Hunter. You have to excuse him. He's half British, but their weather isn't bad enough for him, so he spends most of his time here with us in Maine. He's a historian."

Alec's greeting was little more than a curt nod, and Skylar's gaze flickered to Alec's rough, handsome features and lingered for a moment before returning to Ryan.

"What was your grandmother's name?"

"Agnes Cooper. You gave her friends a jewelry class once."

"I did. I remember her well. She was wonderful." A smile spread across her face, and Ryan saw warmth and humanity beneath the surface beauty.

"She'd love to see you again."

"We should call on her. Em, do you remember her?"

Next to him, Emily stirred. "I wasn't there."

"You must have been." Skylar frowned. "We made necklaces. Brittany helped. Why wouldn't you have been there? We spent the morning on the beach searching for sea glass and then—" She broke off and sent an agonized look of apology toward her friend. "I remember now. You stayed in the cottage. You had a headache."

It was obvious to Ryan it hadn't been a headache that had kept Emily in the cottage, but Skylar's protectiveness made it clear the subject was not up for further discussion.

Emily sat still, but Ryan could feel the tension emanating from her. Her hand rested close to his on the table, and he wanted to slide his fingers over hers and demand that she tell him what was wrong so he could fix it. He wanted to know everything about her. He wanted to know why she'd stayed in the cottage all those years before and not joined her friends on their expedition through the tide pools. He wanted to know why she'd spent three years of her life with a guy who clearly didn't appreciate her and why she'd filled every hour of her day with a job when there were so many more appealing ways of living. And he wanted to rip all the concealing black from her body and explore every inch of her until there wasn't a single part of her he didn't know.

He shifted, distracted by the brutal power of arousal.

And then he saw Lizzy, her hands clasped around a glass, her tumbling hair tucked under the pink baseball cap, and remembered the reason he couldn't follow up on his impulses.

Instead of taking Emily's hand, he picked up his beer, relieved when Kirsti came over to take their order.

Kirsti chatted to Emily, admired Lizzy's hat and tried to draw Alec into conversation with Skylar, an endeavor that earned her a black look.

Skylar ignored it and glanced at the menu. "So what do you recommend?"

Kirsti looked thoughtful. "Depends. Are you hungry?"

"Starving."

Ryan saw the faint gleam of cynical disbelief light Alec's eyes. He'd never met Alec's ex-wife, but the few reports he'd read in the press had given him the impression of a woman for whom the phrase *high maintenance* had probably been invented.

Kirsti leaned forward and pointed. "The clams are good, but my favorite are the homemade crab cakes with dipping sauce. We serve that with French fries and coleslaw but you can switch the fries for a salad if you prefer."

"No way!" Skylar looked horrified. "Fries, please. Lizzy? What do you like?"

"Try the chicken fingers," Kirsti advised. "They are the *best*."

While they waited for the food to arrive, Skylar did most of the talking, her vibrant energy flowing over the group, filling awkward silences, while Lizzy sat watching, her eyes fixed to the gleaming silver bangles that jangled on Skylar's slender arms.

Ryan noticed Lizzy was wearing one, too. It was too big, so she held it with her other hand, as if it were something precious she was determined not to lose.

Emily sat quietly; her eyes were trained on the restaurant, and every time someone new walked through the door she fixed them with her gaze, apparently assessing the threat level. He knew it was no coincidence that she'd given Lizzy the chair facing the water so that her back was to the other diners.

Whatever her feelings about her situation, it was obvious that she took the responsibility seriously.

He suspected she took everything seriously.

He glanced at her profile, taking in the fine bones of her face and the smooth caramel silk of her hair. At first glance it was impossible to believe she was related in any way to Lana Fox. Lana had been fully aware of her assets and prepared to put each and every one on public display in order to guarantee herself a place in the limelight. By contrast, Emily's was a quiet beauty, understated, her discreet manner the very antithesis of her half sister's apparent thirst for attention. From what he'd read, Lana had been addicted to a life of high drama. It seemed to him that Emily had done everything she could to remove drama from her life.

How must it feel for someone who avoided drama like that to assume responsibility for a child she'd never even met?

At least he'd had a close relationship with his siblings. Whatever his feelings on the situation, they'd stuck together as a family.

What Emily had described sounded less like a family and more like a disconnected group of individuals living at the same address.

Kirsti brought lunch, plates heaped high with crab cakes, bowls heaped high with crisp, golden fries.

Fitting five of them around a table intended for four was a squash, and Ryan's knee brushed against Emily's as they shifted to accommodate people and food.

He reached for the salt at the same time as she did, and their fingers tangled.

"Sorry." He murmured the word and disengaged his fingers from hers, but not before several volts of sexual electricity had traveled from her fingers to his.

The salt ended up on the floor.

Across the table, he met Sky's curious gaze.

"So, Ryan—" she sliced into the crab cake on her plate "—what do you do when you're not running this place?"

"I spend time on the water. Isn't that the point of living in Maine?"

Alec finally looked at Skylar. "Where do you live?"

"Manhattan."

Alec's face was blank of expression. "Of course you do."

"Wow." Skylar sat back in her chair and looked at him with a mixture of fascination and indignation. "Do you stereotype everyone you meet?"

Ryan retrieved the salt and handed it to Alec. "He does. You have to forgive him. He's lost his social skills since moving to a remote island. His research means he spends most of his time in the past. I have to force him to interact with live people occasionally."

"Research?"

"The good doctor is writing a naval history. He's much in demand around the world as a lecturer and TV presenter, although I've never understood why the public would want to look at anything that ugly." As expected, Alec didn't rise, but Skylar looked interested.

"Doctor?"

"PhD, so don't show him your war wounds. He only likes blood in the context of history."

Alec put down his fork. "Last time I looked, I was actually sitting here at the table with you. You could include me in the conversation."

"I could, but I'm worried you might lower the mood." Marriage wasn't something Ryan gave much thought to, but spending time with Alec had convinced him that it was better to be single than married to the wrong person. By all accounts his short relationship had more in common with cage fighting than romance.

Skylar pushed her bowl of fries toward Alec. "Help yourself."

"You can't finish them?" Alec threw Ryan a brief "I told you so" look that Skylar intercepted.

"Of course I can finish them, but you look cross, and I'm wondering if your bad mood is because you're hungry. I'm evil when I'm hungry."

Alec tightened his mouth. "I'm not in a bad mood."

Ryan stole one of Skylar's fries. "You should eat your food, Alec. It's good advice."

"If you don't want them, then I'll eat them." Sky pulled the bowl back and ate as if it were her last meal. "These are delicious. How do you make them?"

Ryan thought about the oil. "You probably don't want to know."

"If I didn't want to know I wouldn't have asked."

"They're double fried. It makes the outside extra crispy."

"Full of calories," Alec said pointedly, and Ryan saw Skylar smile.

"That explains why they're so good. You haven't eaten yours. You should. They're incredible."

Alec finally looked properly at Skylar. His gaze traveled from the top of her shiny, glossy hair, down her slender frame and lingered on her fingers, still dipping into her bowl of fries.

She licked her fingers, not provocatively but unselfconsciously, and Ryan felt Alec tense beside him.

"I don't stereotype people. I'm a good judge of character."

"You think you can judge character on external appearance?" Skylar reached for a napkin, her blue eyes cool and her voice low. "Personally I find it dangerous to make assumptions until you've spent time with a person. Take you, for example. If I went on appearances, I'd say you were rude, but you're best friends with Ryan, who is charming, so I'm guessing there's more to you than bad manners. I'm guessing you were hurt in the past, and now you're doing that thing of assuming all women are like the woman who hurt you. That's a way of making sure you live life alone."

A muscle flickered in Alec's jaw. "I'm working on it."

Ryan knew that in Alec's case, the wounds were just too raw for him to be able to see a time when Selina would be nothing more than a mistake in his past.

Alec and Skylar stared at each other, gazes locked in silent battle, and Emily cleared her throat.

"So, you're a maritime historian?"

"He's also a marine archaeologist," Ryan said, "which means we can push him under the water any time we've had enough of him on dry land. Which might be soon, Al."

"Archaeologist?" Emily poured herself a glass of water. "Do you know Brittany?"

Dragging his gaze from Skylar, Alec gave a brief nod. "Yes."

"Don't ever get them together," Ryan advised. "I remember a tedious evening when the two of them talked about nothing but the seafaring history of ancient Minoans. I wanted to drown myself."

Alec pushed his plate away, leaving most of his food untouched. "Is she coming back this summer or is she spending the whole time in Crete?"

"How do you know she's in Crete?"

"We exchange emails. And I read her blog. Her expertise is

Bronze Age weaponry, and there was talk of an exciting find at one of the excavation sites." Alec frowned. "Daggers? Arrowheads?"

Skylar finished her fries. "I've always said that Brittany is the original Lara Croft."

"Does that mean she wears those cute tiny shorts when she's digging?" Ryan leaned forward and stole one of Alec's fries. "I always thought archaeology was boring, but maybe not. I still haven't forgiven her for shooting me in the butt, though, when I was running along the coast path. She'd spent the summer making Cretan arrowheads in Kathleen's garden and decided to test one as I passed."

"Wait a minute—" Emily put her fork down and focused on Alec. "I recognize you, now. You're the Shipwreck Hunter. You made a documentary on the shipwrecks of Maine, and you kayaked the Colorado River with a geologist. I can't remember what it was called. *Adventures through Time* or something. Did you see it, Sky?"

Ryan smiled. "That's the one that got him one-hundred-thousand female followers on Twitter. Or was that the one when you kayaked a section of the Amazon with your shirt off?"

Alec didn't smile, but fortunately Kirsti chose that moment to arrive, clearing plates and offering dessert menus, with a recommendation of warm blueberry pie.

"Did you say blueberry pie?" Skylar sighed wistfully. "Kathleen made the *best* blueberry pie."

"In that case, you should order it, because it's her recipe." Kirsti caught a napkin before it could blow away in the breeze, and the same breeze picked up a strand of Skylar's hair and blew it into Alec's face.

It wrapped itself around him like a golden tentacle, and he jerked away as if he'd been stung.

"Oops, sorry." Skylar scooped her hair over the opposite shoulder and gave Alec a conciliatory smile. "Breezy here. Let me buy you dessert to make up for that moment of unsolicited hair bondage."

The two of them stared at each other, cynic and beauty, violet blue locked with smoldering black.

Feeling as if he were trespassing on an intimate moment, Ryan was about to speak when Alec stood up abruptly.

"Not for me. I have work to do. I'm off to London at the end of the week." He nodded to Emily. "Good to meet you."

To Skylar he said nothing, and Ryan watched as his friend walked out through the restaurant without a backward glance.

Skylar handed the menu back to Kirsti. "I guess he hates dessert." Her voice was calm, but Ryan could see she was upset.

"He hates a lot of things right now. He's going through a rough time. Bad divorce."

"We understand. It's not a problem." It was Emily who spoke, but Ryan noticed that she reached across and squeezed her friend's hand, the bond between the two girls visible to the naked eye.

Skylar gave a quick smile intended to indicate she was fine, and then stared out to sea.

As Kirsti disappeared to the kitchen on a mission to find blueberry pie, Ryan tried to resurrect the conversation.

"So, what are your plans for the afternoon?"

It was Lizzy who answered. "We're going to make jewelry."

For the first time Ryan noticed the pasta necklace around Lizzy's neck. Each piece was painted a different shade of purple and pink and sprinkled with glitter.

"Sounds like fun."

"Can we go on a boat trip?" The innocent question sent a ripple of tension around the table that Ryan detected but didn't understand.

In the end it was Skylar who spoke. "You'll be too busy making jewelry for me to wear next time I visit."

Lizzy wasn't so easily deterred. "I'd like to go on a boat and see the puffins."

"Boats rock and mess up your hair. Maybe we'll go on it next time I'm here," Skylar said quickly. "I'll take you."

Lizzy looked at Emily. "Do boats make you sick?"

"A little." Emily's face was as white as new snowfall, and Ryan knew beyond a shadow of a doubt there was a reason she kept her back to the water.

They shared blueberry pie, and then Kirsti interrupted with a call for Ryan.

He excused himself and walked through to his office, but Kirsti stopped him as he was about to close the door.

"I think Skylar might be The One for Alec." She spoke in a whisper so that whoever was on the phone couldn't hear her.

Ryan laughed. "You have to be kidding me. They almost killed each other."

"I know. I've never seen Alec like that. The chemistry was electric."

"She almost blacked his eye."

"Because he was rude to her and she wasn't having it! Most people are daunted by Alec's intellectual superiority. She squashed him like a bug."

"And that's a good thing?" Baffled, Ryan shook his head. "Skylar isn't his type."

"Ryan, how can such an intelligent guy be so clueless when it comes to relationships? She's *exactly* his type. That's why he was in such a filthy mood. He's used to winning, and he didn't win." She turned away with an exasperated sigh, and Ryan stared after her, trying to picture brooding Alec with free-spirited Skylar.

Exactly his type?

He thought about Emily.

She was responsible for a child, which meant she wasn't his type at all.

CHAPTER SIX

"CALL ME. I want to know how you're both doing." Skylar pulled her case out of the car and took a last breath of sea air. "There are days when I think I could live here. It would be a simpler life. The air is fresh and the light is wonderful. I'd find myself a little studio by the sea where I could paint and make jewelry."

They were standing near the tiny runway, waiting for the Cessna 206 owned by Maine Island Air. The business was the lifeline for islanders needing rapid, easy access to the mainland. It delivered the mail, people and occasionally medical supplies.

Today, Sky was the only passenger.

"Just me and the mail," she said cheerfully, leaning forward to hug Emily. "Ryan is hot by the way, and by *hot* I am talking weapons-grade sex appeal. And I'm willing to bet he doesn't think your breasts are unfortunate. You really should use him to get over Boring Neil."

Emily didn't mention that Ryan had suggested the same thing. Or that, for one crazy minute, she'd actually considered it. "My life is already complicated enough."

Sky checked to see that Lizzy was still safely in the car out of earshot. "Not all complications are bad. Ryan is the whole because he had to "keep an eye on her" all the time. She'd embarrassed him with her appearance, her words, her behavior. She was flirting with everyone. She didn't listen. She finally worked up the courage to walk away after he tried to push her down the stairs in their home one night. But leaving didn't make her safe.

"He's the one who assaulted you in the parking garage?"

She nodded. "I'd gone out with a bunch of people from work to celebrate my birthday. It felt so good to be with people my own age, relaxed and laughing. No one there to criticize my every move. It was the first night I'd felt *free* in ages. It was a new beginning. On the way back to my car, he jumped me and just started punching, over and over, telling me what a whore I was. He broke my cheekbone and five ribs. Punctured a lung. Slammed my head against the cement so hard that I was unconscious for two days."

"Jesus..." Nick's voice was thick with emotion.

"Yeah."

"So the bastard's in jail?"

"Not exactly." She shrugged. "He went to trial, but there was some mysterious mix-up with the evidence or procedure or something, and the judge declared a mistrial. His new trial is coming up. Meanwhile, he's on probation and isn't supposed to leave Milwaukee or contact me in any way. I moved to Cleveland to put some distance between us, but he tracked me down. Got my phone number. My address. Called the office where I worked. Started texting me with threats from a burner phone or something, telling me he was watching me. The DA's office said that wasn't possible, but it freaked me out. Don had never met Aunt Cathy, so I called her, changed my name and came to Gallant Lake."

Nick stared out at the water. She could tell he had a lot of questions, but he was trapped by his promise not to grill her. He was tense. Angry. With her? He said he had a "bad history" with domestic violence victims, but she had no idea what that meant. Police went on a lot of those calls, of course. And they